T0381219

Stefano

AND THE

Tuscan Piazza

Also by Paul Salsini

Fiction

The Ghosts of the Garfagnana: Seven Strange Stories of Haunted Tuscany

"A Tuscan Series":

The Fearless Flag Thrower of Lucca: Nine Stories of 1990s Tuscany

A Piazza for Sant'Antonio: Five Novellas of 1980s Tuscany

The Temptation of Father Lorenzo: Ten Stories of 1970s Tuscany

Dino's Story: A Novel of 1960s Tuscany

Sparrow's Revenge: A Novel of Postwar Tuscany

The Cielo: A Novel of Wartime Tuscany

Nonfiction

Second Start

For Children

Stefano and the Christmas Miracles

Stefano
and the
Tuscan Piazza

All color photos by John Salsini-Tobias

PAUL SALSINI

iUniverse

Stefano and the Tuscan Piazza

Copyright © 2020 Paul Salsini.

All rights reserved. No part of this book may be used or reproduced by any means, graphic, electronic, or mechanical, including photocopying, recording, taping or by any information storage retrieval system without the written permission of the author except in the case of brief quotations embodied in critical articles and reviews.

iUniverse books may be ordered through booksellers or by contacting:

iUniverse
1663 Liberty Drive
Bloomington, IN 47403
www.iuniverse.com
1-800-Authors (1-800-288-4677)

Because of the dynamic nature of the Internet, any web addresses or links contained in this book may have changed since publication and may no longer be valid. The views expressed in this work are solely those of the author and do not necessarily reflect the views of the publisher, and the publisher hereby disclaims any responsibility for them.

ISBN: 978-1-6632-0194-2 (sc)
978-1-6632-0193-5 (e)

Library of Congress Control Number: 2020909539

Print information available on the last page.

iUniverse rev. date: 05/27/2020

For Barbara,

Jim, Laura and Jack

(and my grandfather, Nonno)

AUTHOR'S NOTE

I OFTEN LOOK at a display on a bookshelf next to my chair in our living room. Arranged in a semi-circular fashion, the miniature ceramic buildings form a medieval Tuscan piazza: A church, a bell tower, a palace, a tower, a gate, a well, a variety of houses. The tiny pieces are exquisitely formed and perfectly painted, and I wonder what it would be like to live there.

I purchased the items many years ago in Florence. They were made by "J Carlton by Dominique Gault," which still produces houses and other artifacts representing Paris and Provence, but stopped making the Tuscan line ten years ago.

In one of my musings, I thought of Stefano, the star of my children's book, "Stefano and the Christmas Miracles," and wondered about placing him in that piazza. In fact, he might live in one of the houses. As in the previous book, his grandfather (loosely based on my own Nonno) would tell him stories. Stefano would be transported back to the Middle Ages and discover a whole new world of dukes and peasants, knights and saints, pilgrims and ghosts, glorious feasts and bloody battles.

"Stefano and the Tuscan Piazza" is the result. Enjoy!

MOVE? NEVER!

WHEN THE FIRST BEAMS of sunlight penetrated the lacy curtains and when his mother's coffeepot rumbled in the kitchen below, Stefano slowly woke up and stretched. It would be a good day, he thought. Last night his father had promised to take him to Lucca to get a new videogame. He was tired of his four old ones.

Then he remembered what his father also said. It would help to make up for…for…"We are going to move."

"Move! No!" he shouted so loud that Enrico leaped off the bed.

He turned over and pulled the pillow over his head. "No! No! No!"

Maybe if he went back to sleep he could wipe the thought out of his mind and out of existence. But sleep was impossible. He stared at the ceiling, now decorated with streams of sunlight.

It can't be true, he thought. Why would his Mama and Papa and Nonno want to leave this nice house and move to, where? He remembered: San Ferdinando. Funny name. Who wants to live there?

Needing comfort, he looked for Enrico, who was now cowering in a corner. Stefano grabbed the cat and pulled him under the covers.

He thought some more. How could he convince his parents not to move? They had waited until the last minute to tell him. The move was scheduled for next week. Why?

And then he thought: "I'm not going."

Right. He'd stay here. With Enrico, of course. He could get along. He knew how to fry eggs. He knew how to go to the store and buy milk. He'd be fine. If he got lonesome he'd play with Renzo.

Renzo! He'd stay with Renzo. OK, so they had fights every once in a while, but mostly they got along. Renzo would be happy to have him stay with him. He had to tell him now.

Stefano tore off the covers, raced to the bathroom, threw some water on his face, got dressed and ran downstairs.

"There he is!" his Papa said. "We thought you were going to sleep all day."

His mother kissed the top of his head. "Did you sleep well? We know you're excited about the move."

There was that word again.

"I got to make a phone call," Stefano said.

Going to a table in the hall, he picked up the phone and pressed the buttons.

"Renzo! Guess what! I'm going to live with you!"

Stefano's mother and father stared at each other, their mouths open.

"Yes! Yes, I'm sure. OK, let me talk to your mother."

Stefano's mother and father rolled their eyes.

"Hello? What? Why not? But I thought…Here, I'll let you talk to my mother."

Stefano handed the phone to his Mama.

"*Buongiorno,* Carolina," she said. "I'm so sorry to bother you. No, of course not. No, no, no. I understand. Stefano has a few questions about moving. We didn't tell him until last night, but I'm sure he'll be fine. He's just confused. And I'm sure he'll miss Renzo. Perhaps they can get together sometime. Thank you, Carolina. *Ciao!*"

Taking Stefano by the hand, she led him to the kitchen table where his father and grandfather were finishing their breakfast.

"Now, Stefano," his Papa said, "we know this is a surprise, but as we said last night, we want to move to San Ferdinando. It's such a beautiful village."

"And," his Mama added, "we found a nice house right in the central piazza. You'll have a bigger room where you can keep all your stuff."

"I'm not going."

His father spoke again. "And we'll be closer to Reboli and school. I'll still drive you, and you can wait until I finish my last class and we'll still drive home together."

"I'm not going."

"And," his mother said, "I know there are other boys nearby you can get to know. We saw them playing soccer when we were there the last time. And since this is only June, you can play with them all summer."

"I hate soccer. I'm not going."

"Here, have some toast. I put the marmalade on the way you like it. And we have chocolate milk today!"

"I'm not hungry."

Nonno had remained quiet during all this, soaking some crusty bread in his coffee.

"Stefano," he said, "you know how you like to read about things that happened in the Middle Ages? Well, San Ferdinando goes all the way back there. There are some wonderful old houses and buildings, still kept up. And you should see the piazza! It's nothing like San Domenico. This one has beautiful palazzos and a magnificent tower, and a beautiful church, and…"

"I'M NOT GOING!"

Tears flowed down onto his marmalade toast. He grabbed it and ran to his room.

"Maybe," his mother said, "we should give him something, something besides the videogame?"

"No," his Papa said. "That's enough of a bribe. He's nine years old. He has to learn that he can't have everything he wants. And he's going to love San Ferdinando, right?"

"I hope so."

Nonno got up, cleared the dishes and began washing them.

"Well," he said, "what do you think about driving over there today and let Stefano look at the house, his room, the yard. And then we can walk around the piazza and tell him something about the buildings. That might win him over."

"Good idea! Stefano! Come on down! We're going to take a ride!"

UNA NUOVA CASA

A NEW HOME

STEFANO SCRUNCHED in a corner of the back seat as they left the mountaintop village of San Domenico and headed east. The rolling hills shimmered in shades of green as they descended into the valley, with rows of cypresses marking the farm fields.

"Soon, the sunflowers will be covering all this," Stefano's mother said.

"Nonna always came over here to pick mushrooms," Nonno said. "I don't know how she knew where they were. She could find them when no one else could. Everybody said so."

Nonno pulled out a big white handkerchief from his pocket and wiped his eyes. No one spoke for a long time.

A half hour later, they left the flat plain and began the climb up another mountain. Higher and higher. Round and round. The road narrowed and Papa had to veer to the side when an oncoming car suddenly appeared. Stefano clutched his seatbelt when a gravel truck slid by inches away.

At the top, he saw a sign with an arrow, San Ferdinando. "I'm not staying, I'm not staying, I'm not staying."

As they moved even higher, they saw a scattering of houses amid the farm fields. Then the houses were closer together and mingled with a few shops that had flowers and produce displayed outside.

"And there's our school," Papa said. "I'll be teaching the same classes again. Look at that great soccer field!"

Stefano looked out the window but didn't say anything. They were now in the village.

"And there's a movie theater," Mama said. "We can go there on weekends. We won't have to drive miles and miles to see a movie."

Stefano became more interested. He really wanted to see the new Batman movie.

Papa turned onto Via San Giorgio, then Via Santa Guistina and then a narrow street, Via della Rosa.

"We have to park here," he said. "They don't let cars near the piazza."

They walked down Via della Rosa and entered the piazza under Porta Santa Maria. Clutching brochures, clumps of tourists followed guides carrying umbrellas. A couple of boys tossed a soccer ball, and two gray cats chased each other, but there were no cars.

Staring at all the buildings in the circular piazza, Stefano grabbed his grandfather's hand.

"Nonno! Nonno!" he whispered. "Look! It's just like in my book."

Daily Life in a Medieval Village was Stefano's favorite book and he looked at it every night before he got into bed.

"Yes," his grandfather said, "The piazza in San Ferdinando does look like the pictures in that book. There's the church, and bell tower, and the tall tower, and the houses. And that building over there used to be a palazzo."

"Really? But there are signs for stuff like pizza."

"The insides have been remodeled, and there are some shops on the ground floors, but all the outsides are still the same as they were in the Middle Ages. This is a famous piazza, Stefano, one of the best preserved from the Middle Ages in all of Italy."

"There have been movies made here," Mama said.

"And," Papa said, "there's a guy who makes tourist programs for television, Rick Steves, who did something about it a few years ago. And it was featured in the book *The Most Beautiful Villages in Tuscany.*"

The family moved to the middle, near a well, and Stefano turned around and around, looking at all of the buildings. His eyes grew wider with every turn.

"Wow!" he shouted. "Wow! Wow!"

Papa led his family to the small house next to the gate. Three stories tall with a red tile roof, it had a door on the ground level and another up a small flight of stairs to the second level. Pink roses rising from a flower box almost covered a small window at the top, and a tricolor medieval flag hung from a larger window next to it.

"This is our new home, Stefano," his mother said. "Like it?"

"This one? Really? It's so cool! Wow! Wow!"

Papa dug out a large iron key and opened the door. Unlike the exterior, the rooms inside were greatly modernized.

"Look, Stefano, this living room is huge! You can have your own corner over there and watch television and play your videogames. And look at this dining room. It's big enough for a table to seat eight people. And the kitchen! All new appliances, or pretty new anyway."

He led the group up the stairs, Nonno coming last with his cane. They saw the bedroom for Mama and Papa and the one for Nonno, and finally Stefano's.

The boy was overwhelmed. "Cool!"

"Look," his Mama said, "we can put your bed here and there's even space for a little bed for Enrico."

"He'll still sleep with me."

"And you can have a desk, Stefano! You can do your drawing and coloring there, and, of course, your homework. And you can have a bookcase for your books and your cars and trucks and videogames."

"And," his Papa said, "they left a telescope by the window. You can look up at the stars. I'll tell you their names."

Nonno pointed to the garden down below in the back. "I can have tomatoes again. It's been so long. We used to have them at our house before I moved in with you. And lettuce. And beans. And broccoli."

Stefano wandered around the room, touching the walls, looking out the window. He examined the telescope. He opened the door to the closet, went inside and closed the door.

"Where's Stefano?" his Papa asked loudly.

"I don't know," his Mama said. "He was here a minute ago."

"Well, we have go," Papa said. "He'll have to find his own way home. Come on, Nonno."

Laughing, Stefano burst out out of the closet. "Fooled you! Fooled you!"

His parents smiled, and said they'd better get back home. They could explore the piazza some other day.

"But maybe there would be time for a *gelato*?" Nonno said.

"*Cioccolato*!" Stefano cried.

PIAZZA SANT'AUGUSTINO

PIAZZA SANT'AUGUSTINO

WITH THE HELP of Papa's friends who had trucks, the move from San Domenico to San Ferdinando was accomplished in one long day. Everyone was exhausted that night, and Stefano was so tired his mother had to practically brush his teeth.

When he got under the covers, though, with Enrico stretched out at the bottom, he was suddenly wide awake. He tried to count the stars out his window.

"Come see the stars!" he cried. "There's zillions of them!"

"Go to sleep, Stefano," his father called out.

"*Buona notte*!" Stefano cried.

"*Buona notte*!" Nonno called from his room.

"*Buona notte*!" Mama and Papa called from theirs.

"*Buona notte*!" Stefano called again.

"OK, that's enough," Papa said. "Go to sleep, Stefano."

"*Buona notte, Enrico!*" Stefano whispered.

Papa turned to his wife. "You know, he hasn't mentioned Renzo once."

"I hope he can make friends here," Mama said.

The family spent the next four days unpacking, arranging and rearranging. Stefano stayed at his desk for hours, drawing one thing or another, and then more time at his bookshelf where he moved his cars and trucks and videogames endlessly. He sorted his books in alphabetical order, then according to size and then according to subject.

When he looked out the window, he could see his grandfather carefully putting in the little tomato plants he had purchased from a farmer outside of town. When he looked in his telescope at night, he could discover stars he had never seen before.

"Papa! Mama! Come see! I think it's the Big Dipper!" His mother and father had invariably just fallen asleep.

He loved to explore the house, finding nooks and crannies stuffed with odd things like vases and jewelry and carvings. Some looked very old, and he imagined that a few had been there since the Middle Ages.

"You could be right," his Papa said. "We'll never know for sure, and we can only imagine."

Stefano became very excited when he saw the number "1457" carved in a piece of plaster on the wall near his bedroom.

"Papa! Mama! Nonno! Do you think this house was really built in 1457?"

"Maybe," Nonno said. "This might have been a barn or something then."

"Really! Wow! How cool!"

Enrico also explored the house, running up and down the stairs and finding places to hide. The tiny corner under the second-floor landing became a favorite spot, and Stefano put an old towel there for him to sleep on.

The family soon discovered that there were some elements that reflected the house's ancient history. The plumbing was erratic, with water sometimes gushing out of the kitchen faucet and other times trickling. The electrical wiring seemed to depend on whims. Lights went on, or off, with no one near a switch. After a rainstorm, there was scurrying to find rags and pails to stem the leaks from the tile roof and the windows. Papa called the village roofer who was understandably very busy.

"Maybe that's why the house was on the market for so long," Papa told Mama, "and why we got it so cheap."

Unlatching a wooden door, the family found a small room almost hidden on the third floor and decided to use it for storage. On a shelf, Nonno placed the box containing their most treasured possession: the forty-piece *presepio* that was brought out every December. Each night Nonno told Stefano the stories of many of the figures who went to Bethlehem to see the Baby Jesus. It was the boy's favorite time of the year.

Only Piazza Sant'Augustino and the buildings on its circumference dated from the Middle Ages. Beyond, the houses were relatively new—the oldest only a hundred years old—and the rest of the village reflected modern times. A computer store was on one street, a gas station on another, a new supermarket on a third. There was a modern church, Saint Agatha's, and a sleek elementary school that Stefano would attend in the fall.

Each evening, many of the villagers came out for the *la passeggiata*, and the family joined them in strolling around the piazza. It soon became a tradition for Mama and Papa to walk some more while Nonno and Stefano went to the *Gelateria* for ice cream. There were endless choices—tiramisu, hazelnut, pistachio, lemon, banana, strawberry, peach, coconut, strawberry, butter pecan. Nonno deliberated but usually chose the lemon while Stefano always said, "*Cioccolato!*"

They found a bench and one night Stefano tried to count all the stones in the massive gate.

"As you can see," Nonno said, "Porta Santa Maria was the main entrance to Piazza Sant'Augustino, so it had to be guarded well."

"What's that window for?"

"A guard was on lookout day and night."

"Why?"

"In medieval times there were lots of enemies. One village against another. One army fighting another. The roads were very dangerous."

"Why does the top look like that?"

"Those pieces standing up are called crenels, and the roof is called crenellated. Soldiers stood on the roof and were able to shoot arrows at the enemy through the empty spaces."

"Do all Italian cities have piazzas, Nonno?"

"Most of them, I think. There's a famous one in Venice, right near the lagoon and with a huge cathedral. There are many in Rome, like the Piazza Navona or Campo de' Fiori, which means field of flowers, and of course, the huge piazza in front of St. Pater's. In Siena it's called the Campo and there's a big horse race there twice a year. And in Florence, there's a bloody soccer game every June in the piazza in front of the Santa Croce cathedral."

"Bloody? Really?"

"I'll tell you about that some other day. Now let's just talk about piazzas. It seems like even small villages like this one have a piazza. They're an Italian tradition but their history goes back centuries and centuries.

"You see, people have always wanted to be together. That's just our nature. So in prehistoric times they probably gathered on a hilltop or a meadow for a celebration. Then the Greeks and Romans built circular spaces for games and plays. They called them amphitheaters. And soon there were markets in the spaces.

"In the Renaissance there was a great show of power, and so the piazzas were surrounded by palazzos and towers and churches."

"Like here?"

"Yes. In a small way. You see the church dedicated to Saint Zita, and the bell tower. Across the way is an old palace. And over there that building used to be where travelers stayed. So many beautiful buildings. And every one of them has a story. Next time, I'll start telling you about them."

"Can I have another *gelato*, Nonno?"

"No."

ALBERGO SANT'ANNA

ALBERGO SANT'ANNA

THE FAMILY quickly became used to life in their new village. Papa spent one or two nights a week at a sports bar watching Juventus and Fiorentina matches on television with new friends. Mama enjoyed shopping in the variety of shops outside the piazza and she joined a book club that was reading, and re-reading, Elena Ferrante's Neapolitan novels.

Nonno worked in his garden and often just sat reading or smoking his pipe under one of the three peach trees in the back yard. Despite the heat of the Tuscan summer, he invariably wore his customary three-piece black suit, with the vest tightly buttoned and adorned with his gold watch chain. His red-and-gold tie was carefully knotted, and his fedora allowed a few strands of white hair to show in the back. He held on to his ebony cane with its shiny lion's head at the top.

Stefano mostly stayed in his room until one day, Mama answered the doorbell to find a young curly haired boy.

"Does a boy live here now?" he asked.

"Yes, yes he does. What's your name?"

"Vincenzo."

"Stefano! There's a boy named Vincenzo here to see you."

Stefano came up behind his mother.

"Want to play soccer?" Vincenzo asked.

After a little hesitation: "OK."

Stefano's mother hurried upstairs to tell her husband. "Stefano's made a friend!"

Eating their ice cream cones on their favorite bench that night, Nonno wanted to know about his grandson's new friend.

"Do you like him?" he asked.

"He's OK," Stefano said. "He has six videogames. Nonno, tell me about the history of this village."

"Well," Nonno began, "San Ferdinando has existed for hundreds and hundreds of years. First it was just a group of farms, and then it became a tiny village and grew and grew. In medieval times they built this beautiful piazza because the town was famous as one of the stops that pilgrims made on their way to Rome or other holy places."

"I've heard about pilgrims, but I don't understand why they made those trips."

"In those times," Nonno said, "the Catholic Church had a bigger role in people's lives than it does today. Faith wasn't an abstract idea, but it was part of everyday life. People built great churches in many cities and they went to pray in them.

"Many times, they gathered in groups, sometimes large, sometimes small, and traveled to a sacred shine so that they could pray there. Sometimes the shrines were famous because miracles supposedly happened there, maybe people were cured of cancer or something. Or sometimes people went to ask forgiveness for their sins. Or maybe they had special reasons, like wanting to have children."

"Why was San Ferdinando a stop?"

"Mainly because it was about midway between two other stops. There were many stops because some of the pilgrims were going to Rome and some were even going farther, to the Holy Land. Some of these people were traveling thousands of miles, and most of them were on foot. So they had to stop many many times. San Ferdinando was the last stop before Lucca."

"Where did they stay?"

"See that building over there, the tall building with the blue shutters? It used to be a hotel called Albergo Sant'Anna. It was one of maybe a dozen places in San Ferdinando—they were called inns then—but all the others are gone. No one could take care of them. Albergo Sant'Anna was popular because the food was always good, the rooms were clean and the people who ran the place were kind and understanding. So word got around that people should stay at Albergo Sant'Anna.

"I bet the pilgrims were tired."

"Exhausted. They could only travel during the day because there were so many dangers. They had to be on the lookout for thieves and kidnappers and outlaws who would descend from the hills and attack them. And there were also wolves and boars and other wild animals on the way."

"Boars?"

"Yes, boars."

"Wild boars?"

"Yes."

"I'll never go on a pilgrimage."

"And also, there was a lot of disease and illness along the way. They didn't have toilets or sanitation back then, and so germs were spread and…"

"Nonno, I don't want to hear all this."

Stefano stared at the old building for a long time.

"I like all the windows."

"You see that window on the top, at the right?"

"Yes."

"That's the room where Caterina and her daughter stayed."

"Who?"

"I'll tell you the story. It seems that in the Sixteenth century, around 1520, there was a young woman named Caterina Nelli who lived in a village west of San Martino in Freddana. Her husband had drowned at sea and she was trying to raise their daughter Rosa all by herself. When Rosa was about nine years old, about the same as you are now, she developed a terrible illness. She was so weak, she had to stay in bed most of the time. Nobody knew what was wrong with her.

"When Rosa got a little better, Caterina decided to take her on a pilgrimage. She found a sort of wagon and put Rosa in it and started off. They got to the first stop, then the second stop and then the third stop. All along the way, the other pilgrims watched over her and prayed with Caterina and gave her some of their food and even took turns pulling her cart. Caterina was very grateful."

"Nonno, where were they going? Was it going to take a long time?"

"Ah, I'm glad you asked. They were going to Lucca—you know where that is—and they were going to pray for a miracle before the beloved Volto Santo."

"What's that?"

"Now I'm going to tell you a wonderful story. If you don't believe it, that's up to you. But remember what I've always said. Sometimes it's best to trust in God and just believe. OK, here's the story.

"After Jesus' death, his good friend Nicodemus carved a wooden statue representing Christ's body. He had completed everything except the face before he fell asleep. When he awoke, the face had been completed. He was sure it was done by an angel."

"What?"

"Somehow, the statue was lost for seven centuries, and then a boat carried it to the port of Ortonovo. That's a town on the western coast of Italy. The statue was in a boat that didn't have sails, and it didn't have a crew."

"What?"

"It didn't have a crew. That's what I said. Then it was carried in a cart to Lucca. The cart was towed by oxen but it didn't have a driver."

"Nonno!"

"It didn't have a driver. First it was placed in the Church of San Frediano, but now it's in the Cathedral of San Martino. The people of Lucca revere the statue and it's carried through the streets in a procession every September. The next time we go to Lucca maybe we can go to see it."

"Really?"

"But back to our story about Caterina. During the Middle Ages Lucca became known for having the statue of the Volto Santo, and it became a regular stopping point for pilgrims. It was even designated as a stop on the Via Francigena, which was the official route between a city called Canterbury in England and Rome.

"Caterina was very anxious to get to Lucca and pray before the Volto Santo, but something terrible happened after they left San Martino in Freddana and before they arrived here in San Ferdinando. A band of outlaws, about a dozen, suddenly burst down from the hills and attacked the pilgrims. The other pilgrims ran away, some of them even plunged into a river nearby. But Caterina couldn't go very far with Rosa in her cart and three of the ruffians attacked her. They threw her to the ground and grabbed the purse that she tied around her waist. It had all the money she had in the world, every *florin*.

"After the outlaws had fled, the other pilgrims came back and found Caterina holding Rosa. Both of them were sobbing. 'Don't cry,' the pilgrims said, 'don't cry.'"

"And they all took out their purses and gave her some money, but it wasn't enough. When they got to San Ferdinando they went to the Albergo Sant'Anna and Caterina explained the situation. 'Don't worry,' the innkeeper said. 'You are welcome to stay. We have a nice room on the top floor.'

"So Caterina and Rosa stayed in that room and on the next day they joined the others to go to Lucca."

"Did she pray before this statue?"

"Yes, and that's the best part of this story. Caterina and Rosa got to Lucca and to the cathedral. Caterina pulled the cart even on the marble floor right up to where the Volto Santo was placed. She knelt down and prayed. Suddenly, the statue glowed with a soft light. And Rosa got out of the cart and hugged her mother. She was cured.

"And that's not the end of the story. The other pilgrims went on to Rome, but Caterina and Rosa returned to San Ferdinando to thank the innkeeper again. The innkeeper was so impressed that he not only invited Caterina to stay in that room again, but he said that if she wanted to, she could stay as long as she wanted. He said the inn needed another person to greet pilgrims and care for them. So Caterina stayed there the rest of her life, and Rosa grew up and married a young man in San Ferdinando and had four wonderful children."

Stefano thought about this for a long time. "Nonno, is this a true story?"

"Remember what I told you, Stefano. Sometimes you have to trust in God."

THE *PASTICCERIA*

THE *SBANDIERATORI*

ONE MORNING, the family was awakened by the sound of boisterous crowds that had surged through the gate and were out on the piazza singing the Italian national anthem.

Fratelli d'Italia,
L'Italia s'è desta;
Dell'elmo di Scipio
S'è cinta la testa.
Dov'è la Vittoria?
Le porga la chioma;
Ché schiava di Roma
Iddio la creò.

Brothers of Italy,
Italy has awoken,
With Scipio's helmet
Binding her head.
Where is Victory?
Let her bow down,
For God has made her
Rome's slave.

The family rushed outside.
"Why are they singing, Nonno?"
"The *Sbandieratori dei Borghi e Sestieri Fiorentini* are coming!

"Wow! What does that mean?"

"It means the flag throwers from a village near Florence."

"What! What are flag throwers?"

"You'll see. We're lucky. They only come here to perform once a year and this is the day."

The crowd suddenly roared as they heard the sounds of drums in the distance. The drums became louder. Soon, they were joined by trumpets playing fanfares. Everyone turned to the Porta Santa Maria.

"Here they come!" everyone shouted.

Eight drummers entered Piazza Sant'Augustino through the gate first. They were teenage boys wearing medieval clothing, or at least a modern version of medieval clothing: silk tunics that were deep blue on one side and white on the other and emblazed with a gold sun on their chests. Their tights were also blue and white and they wore blue leather boots.

The drummers marched around the edge of the piazza, then spread out next to the church.

The trumpeters followed, six older boys and young men. Always a crowd favorite, they circled the square blaring their horns and then stood next to the drummers.

There was a long pause and for a moment some people wondered if the exhibition was over.

Suddenly, twelve men, some young, others in their sixties, raced headlong into the piazza. Each carried a huge flag with the same blue and white colors and with a fleur-de-lis.

The horde roared, the drums sounded and the trumpets blared as the flag bearers trotted around the edge of the piazza once, then twice, then three times. The crowd yelled even louder. "*Sbandieratori! Sbandieratori!*"

Vincenzo came running over.

"Do you see them? Do you see them?"

"Yes! Yes!"

Both boys covered their ears and began jumping up and down.

The flag bearers now lined up next to the trumpeters so that every building on the northern half of the piazza had a member of the *sbandieratori* in front of it.

"Look!" Stefano cried. "There's a guy with a trumpet in front of our house."

Another long pause.

"What are they going to do now?" Stefano asked his grandfather.

"Just wait."

Four of the flag throwers slowly approached the well in the middle of the piazza. They bowed to each other and tossed the flags in the air. The crowd cheered. After catching them, they threw the flags higher. Then higher still. Higher.

They threw them to each other, each time getting the flags higher so that soon they were as high as the bell tower. Then they stopped, bowed, and retreated to their places along the side. The throng wanted more.

Another four did the same, then the last four. Stefano and Vincenzo couldn't get enough of this. They wormed their way to the front of the crowd, and bounced up and down in rhythm with the flags. The drummers drummed and the trumpeters trumpeted.

Now six of the flag throwers came forward. Not only did they throw the flags in the air to each other in a round robin, they also slid them under their feet, caught them in their arms and waved them over their heads.

The crowd went crazy. More drum beats, more blaring trumpets.

After the second six duplicated, and even bettered, the first six, all twelve of the flag throwers began the grand finale, throwing the flags up and over and down and around, never failing to catch one even from across the piazza. After elaborate bows, and with the drums and trumpets louder than ever, they all ran round the perimeter and ran off under the Porta Santa Maria.

Two minutes later, answering the calls of the crowd, they returned to bound around the edge and then stopped to bow again. The leader, a man in his early sixties, called to the crowd: "*Grazie, molto grazie!*"

The mass of people surged and soon everyone was vying to talk to a flag thrower and to take selfies. This went on for quite a while until one of the *sbandieratori* caught sight of Stefano and Vincenzo.

"Are you the young men who were enjoying our performance so much?"

The boys could only nod.

"Well, *grazie*! Would you like to be a s*bandieratori* when you grow up?"

Both nodded wildly.

"Well, we have a school, and you can enter when you are twelve years old. You look like that already, right?"

They shook their heads.

"No? Then you must be eleven? No? Ten? No? Nine?"

Stefano and Vincenzo nodded.

"Nine years old! You are big for nine. You could have fooled me! Well, I'll give you something to practice on. It's small, but you can throw it in the air and get the feel of it."

The man went to a nearby table and returned with two flags, identical to the *sbandieratori,* but about a fourth in size.

"What do you say, Stefano?" Nonno asked.

Stefano could hardly get the words out. "*Grazie! Molto grazie*!"

Enjoying their ice cream that night, Nonno told Stefano the history of flag throwers, how they dated back to the Middle Ages.

"A soldier held a flag aloft in front of the troops as they went into battle," he said, "And if the soldier was wounded, he would throw the flag to another soldier. And that began the tradition. We were lucky to be here today, right, Stefano?"

"I wish I could see them again."

"They'll be back next year. San Ferdinando used to have a group of flag throwers. The *Sbandieratori della Santa Zita di San Ferdinando*. They made their headquarters in that building over there, where the *Pasticceria* is. See the gold sun at the top? That was their symbol."

"Were they good?"

Nonno chuckled. "Wait for the *Festa della Santa Zita di San Ferdinando* in August."

"Why are you laughing, Nonno?"

"You'll see."

PALAZZO DEL DUCA DI SAN FERDINANDO

PALAZZO DEL DUCA DI SAN FERDINANDO

EVERY NIGHT, Stefano pored over the pages of *Daily Life in a Medieval Village*, imagining himself in the buildings of the piazza so long ago. Maybe he would go to the top of the gate and shoot arrows down at the enemy. Or perhaps he would hang out at the hotel and wait for the pilgrims. Or he would march around the piazza and toss his *sbandieratori* flag in the air.

He actually did that, and hoped that no one noticed when the flag fell.

One night, he asked his grandfather about a tall building with fancy windows.

"Ah, that, Stefano, was once the most famous building in the village, the *Palazzo del Duca di San Ferdinando*."

"A palace? It doesn't look much like a palace."

"Not anymore. But when it was new, and for a couple of centuries after, it was the main building in San Ferdinando and in all of the countryside."

"Really?"

"You see, in the Middle Ages and afterward, Italy was divided into many territories. Some were big, but many were small. There were rulers in each of them and there were many wars. The leader of one place wanted more territory so he'd have his army invade the one next door and they'd fight and sometimes the leader won and sometimes not.

"Well, in the 1500s, San Ferdinando conquered two neighboring territories and it became quite large. It was established as a dukedom, and the king of Italy named a wealthy man, Carlo, as the first duke. He and his wife, whose name was Lucia, presided over the village.

"Duke Carlo and Lucia built this beautiful palace to show how important San Ferdinando was. Inside, there was a great hall where Carlo and Lucia greeted their guests. There was a ballroom with an inlaid floor and heavy curtains and paintings. There were kitchens and pantries and larders and butteries. And lavatories and of course bedrooms. The top floor was a playroom for the children.

"And you see those two windows on the second floor? They would open the windows on special occasions, like feasts, and the duke and duchess would wave to the crowds down below."

Stefano made a gesture like he was waving to the crowds.

"The duke designed this great coat of arms with the typical symbols of his reign. There was a shield, an arrow, a lion, a book and other things. He had it placed on a big silk banner that hung in the great hall.

"Now, the duke and duchess had three daughters and then they had a son, Roberto. When the duke died, Roberto would succeed him.

"Nonno," Stefano interrupted, "why would Roberto succeed his father when there were daughters who were older?"

"Good question, Stefano! There was at that time a system called primogeniture. Primo-gen-iture. That means that the eldest son always succeeded the father. If the first son died, then the next son was in line, and so on, no matter if there were daughters who were older."

Stefano pondered this for a while. "It doesn't seem right to me. If makes it sound like girls weren't as important as boys."

"Which isn't true, of course. It's taken a long time for people to realize what a problem this is, and we're still trying to get things right. Anyway, the duke wanted to be certain that Roberto would succeed him, and he was very protective of his son. But then something terrible happened, or at least the duke thought so."

"What?"

"Roberto fell in love with a poor girl from another village."

"So?"

"In those days, it was important for people to marry within what they called their 'class.' Rich people just didn't marry poor people."

"Not even if they were in love?"

"No. The duke discovered that Roberto and the girl, Elena, were meeting in secret halfway between San Ferdinando and her village, San Paolo. The duke called his son in and they had a big fight. Roberto said he loved Elena and wanted to marry her. The duke got so mad he sent Roberto off to fight in one of the wars San Ferdinando was involved in then.

"Roberto was away for two years and Duke Carlo thought for sure he would have forgotten about Elena when he returned, but no. Roberto was still in love and the duke heard that he was meeting with the girl again. So he sent his son off to another war."

"And Roberto came back still in love with Elena, right?"

"Right. So off he went to another war, but this time, he came back very badly wounded. In fact, they had to amputate his left leg."

"Ouch!"

"The duke and duchess nursed him back to health and they thought that surely there would no longer be a romance between Roberto and Elena. But somehow Elena found out about this and managed to sneak into the palace, pretending she was a servant girl. She met Roberto and they hugged and kissed. Duke Carlo and Lucia realized they couldn't control their son's emotions any longer so they let Roberto and Elena get married. And when the duke died, Roberto became the duke and Elena became the duchess."

"Is that the end of the story?"

"Almost. Roberto and Elena had four children and the children had children but, like a lot of children, they didn't want to live with their parents anymore. They moved away and over the centuries there were lots of descendants scattered all over. So there are heirs all over Italy and in other countries, too, but nobody knows where they are.

"The children and the grandchildren and all the other relatives divided all the furnishings in the palace. One family took some paintings, another took the beautiful curtains, another the fine china. The furniture went all over. I heard that some of the beds and chairs ended up in England. But no one seems to know what happened to one piece."

"Which one?"

The banner with the coat of arms. That would be priceless today. It would be an authentic link to the first royal family of San Ferdinando. Anyway, eventually the village took over the palace and turned it into a school for children from all over the area, including those from San Paolo. And it still offers classes today, in computers, in foreign languages, in cooking. All sorts of things. Someday, you can take classes there."

"Maybe."

IL POZZO

THE BLOODY GAMES

STEFANO WAS NOT having a good day. He had gotten up early so he could practice flag throwing in the piazza before his friend Vincenzo came over. But it was the worst practice he'd ever had, with the flag falling on the ground half the time and hitting him in the face or arms or butt the other times. He could swear he heard some nuns snickering as they went to early Mass.

Then Vincenzo turned up, bearing his flag from the *sbandieratori* performance. Putting on a show for Stefano, he marched around in a circle with the flag over his shoulder, then tossed it in the air—and caught it—over and over.

Stefano couldn't stand looking at him and ran to his room. Nonno found him later with his head under his pillow.

"Not feeling good?"

"No."

"Have a fight with your friend?"

"No."

"Would you like to play with him again?"

"No. I hate him."

"I thought maybe a *gelato* would cheer you up, but probably not. I'll see you later."

"Wait!"

As they sat on their bench with their ice creams, Stefano watched the two resident cats chase each other around the piazza. He threw them a stick, which fell into the well.

"Nonno," he asked, "how come there's a well in the middle of the piazza?"

"*Il pozzo*? It's there because the stream of water from the Serchio River is underneath. Want to look?"

They walked over to the well, where there was a small line of children waiting to dip a cup into the water. When they got to the edge, Nonno urged his grandson to look down.

"Can you see the bottom?"

"I can't even see the middle. This must be very deep."

"They say it's two thousand feet deep."

"Wow."

"Have a taste?"

Stefano dipped the cup into the well.

"It's cold!"

"That's because the well is so deep. There's a story about the well, but I think you're too young to hear it."

"No I'm not! I'm nine years old! I'm gonna be ten in September! Nonno, please!"

"Well, all right. Take a look into the well before we start."

They returned to their bench and Nonno began his story.

"First, you should know that San Ferdinando, like many small towns and villages at that time, wanted to be like the big cities, or at least look like them. This piazza, for example, was modeled after one in Lucca, the Piazza dell'Anfiteatro. The flag throwers that we saw? Oh, so many places had them, it would be hard to say which place was the real model for the ones here.

"Well, in the Renaissance, the city of Florence began a tradition of what they called 'historic soccer,' *calcio storico*. Actually, they copied it from an ancient game called *harpustum* from the Roman Empire, which was copied from a Greek game. Anyway, the games were popular because they were so violent and bloody. The crowds loved it. They cheered whenever a player had to be carried off the field because he was so badly hurt."

"Yuck."

"Florence discovered the game in the late Fifteenth century, and it was played in the winter on the frozen Arno River, and then it became very popular in the Sixteenth century. It was played off and on after that until the Kingdom of Italy in 1930 reorganized the game under Benito Mussolini."

"Mussolini? I thought he was a bad guy."

"Well, some people might think *calcio storico* is not a good thing. In fact, maybe a lot of people."

"It was still bloody?"

"Oh, yes. Young men played it in the streets and in squares and piazzas. Then it was organized in the piazza in front of the Church of Santa Croce. And it's still held there, in the third week of June every year.

"Are there teams?"

"There are teams from each quarter in the city, which are named after the churches there. One for Santa Croce, one for Santa Maria Novella, one for Santo Spirito and one for San Giovanni. They wear different colors and there are twenty-seven men on each team. If one gets hurt or does something so bad that he's expelled, he's not replaced. But he'd have to do something really bad to be expelled."

"Like what?"

"Well, such things as punching, kicking, tackling, wrestling, elbowing and choking were allowed by the rules."

"They can do that?"

"Yes. So you can imagine what was not allowed. For example, kicks to the head were banned."

"Oh."

"Men have been killed, Stefano. The aim is to get the ball into the goal by whatever means."

"And people come to watch this?"

"We don't understand why, Stefano. There must be something down deep in us that encourages us to watch this stuff. Would you go?"

"No. Well, maybe. No, I don't think so. I wouldn't want to see somebody killed."

"And what does this have to do with San Ferdinando?" Nonno asked. "Well, as I said, the village liked to copy what other places were doing. So in the last century, the men who ran this village decided that they would have a *calcio storico,* too. They rounded up some big burly men and put on a match right here in this piazza. The men attacked each other, but it wasn't very fierce and the mobs jeered. The next time they began tearing each other's shirts off and punching. The third time there was blood all over. If you look real close over there in front of the church, you can still see some stains."

Stefano went to look and was delighted to report that he really did see bloodstains.

"Well," Nonno said, "a few weeks after that match, this all came to a halt. There was a young man on one team, I think his name was Stefano…"

"Really?"

"And his best friend was on the other team, I seem to remember that his name was Vincenzo or something like that, and…"

"Nonno! You're making this up!"

"Well, the team that Stefano was on got really rough and they were throwing the other team around and then one of them had an idea. They would throw this Vincenzo into the well."

"No! He'd drown."

"Exactly. So this Stefano, all by himself, started slugging his fellow team members so they wouldn't capture Vincenzo. The crowd booed, of course, but Stefano didn't care. Finally, he and Vincenzo walked arm in arm out of the piazza, right through Porta Santa Maria over there, and that was the end of *calcio storico* in San Ferdinando. There was never another match."

"What happened to Stefano and Vincenzo?"

"They stayed friends. A few years later they married two sisters."

"Nonno, sometimes I think you make these stories up."

"Me?"

THE *GELATERIA*

MARKET DAY

AS USUAL, disagreements between Stefano and Vincenzo were soon forgotten, and Stefano visited his friend's house that night for more videogame competition. That was good because the next day, Thursday, had quickly become the highlight of the boys' month and they wanted to go together.

Held on the second Thursday of every month, Market Day in San Ferdinando was known far and wide as one of the best venues for food and merchandise in all of Tuscany. People came from Lucca, Pisa and sometimes even Florence to dicker and haggle with the vendors and leave with car trunks full of fresh vegetables and the odd antique or whatnot that had been salvaged from a barn or garage and put on display.

Stefano and Vincenzo didn't care much about the produce. It was more fun to scatter through the stalls and tables that were set up all over the piazza and see what they could pilfer from unsuspecting farmers. Then it became a game of hide and seek as the vendors chased the boys from behind one stall to another. When their pockets were full, they ran behind the church and devoured apples and peaches and biscotti and didn't leave any room for supper.

One of the vendors, Signora Genovesi, a woman so stout she could never have given chase, always held an apple out to Stefano as soon as he approached. He didn't think that was much fun.

That night, Stefano asked his grandfather about the history of market days. They had watched another episode of *Il Commissario Montalbano* in which the inspector had visited a market during an investigation of a murder.

"Market Days were different when Duke Carlo and Lucia reigned over the village," Nonno said as he picked up the half-finished basket he was making out of reeds. Although he liked to sit in the garden during the day, he'd taken up the hobby years ago for something to do at night. Baskets of varying sizes—some round, some oblong—decorated the home and were welcomed gifts for friends and neighbors. Enrico liked to take naps in the one next to the fireplace.

Stefano sat crossed-leg beside him on the floor and handed him the reeds and scissors.

"It was simpler in those days," Nonno continued. "It was mostly just for farmers. They brought in not only lettuce and beets and cucumbers, but also things you'll only find in Italy—*finocchio,* or fennel, *cicoria,* or chicory, *carciofi,* or artichokes, or *scarola,* a kind of head lettuce.

"Or even *agretti*. You know that one, Stefano. It's a vegetable that looks like hair. In fact, it's Italian nickname is *barba di frate* or friar's beard. Your mother sautés it with oil and garlic and puts it on pasta."

"It does look like hair," Stefano said. "I never thought of that."

"Anyway, there was great competition among the farmers then. Who had the best *cicoria,* who had the best *scarola.* It got so bad that sometimes there were fist fights. 'I have better *agretti* than you do!' 'No, you don't! I do!'"

Stefano began to laugh.

"It wasn't funny. One time a farmer put some deadly weeds in another farmer's *cicoria.* Luckily, the farmer's wife discovered it or someone would have gotten very sick."

"Why was the market so important?" Stefano wanted to know.

"Because all these farmers were very poor. They were tenant farmers and they had to give a big part of what they earned to their landlords, so they didn't have much left. They depended on the sales they made on market days to last them for the week. And if the weather was bad, or if there was some other disaster and they couldn't sell their produce, well, the whole family didn't eat much for days. Anyway, I think about those early days every time we go to the *Gelateria* for *gelato.*"

"Really?"

"The *Gelateria* is small, but it was very important in the days of Duke Carlo. Lucia told her husband how she had seen a farmer snatch some *finocchio* from another farmer and try to sell it as his own. The other farmer saw him and they were about to come to blows when some big burly farmers pulled them apart. Duke Carlo said, 'Well, that's enough' and he went down to settle things.

"He stood in front of the building that is now the *Gelateria* and he decreed that every farmer had to get a permit from an inspector inside and that they had to show their merchandise. The permit wasn't expensive, but it wasn't cheap either, so the farmers knew they had to have good vegetables and fruit and whatever else they were selling."

"Sounds like a plan."

"It all worked out well. The farmers did what they were told and the village used the money from the fees to put a big sign on the building. You know where it says *Gelateria*?"

"Yes."

"Originally, it said '*Giorno del mercato,*' or Market Day, and soon people from other villages started coming because they thought that any event with that big a sign must be pretty good. As they say, 'It pays to advertise.'"

"Is that what they say?"

"Yes. Want to go get a *gelato* tomorrow?

"*Cioccolato*!"

VECCHIO MULINO

WITCHES AND DEVILS AND GHOSTS

WAITING TO GO TO VINCENZO'S, Stefano was eating a sandwich on the steps in front of his house when a tourist group stopped at the old building next door. The tour guide, a slim woman who may have been a college student, pointed her umbrella at the building.

"Now this," Stefano heard her say, "as you can see from the sign, is an old mill, *Vecchio Mulino*. During the Middle Ages, this is where farmers from the countryside brought their grain and it was ground into wheat and then into loaves of bread. Like today, the bread then was long and hard and crusty."

"And very good!" one of the tourists shouted.

"Anyway," the guide continued, "I wanted to stop here because there are some strange legends about this building."

The tourists perked up, and so did Stefano.

"It seems—and you don't have to believe this—that ghosts are sometimes seen around the old machinery, which of course has been abandoned for many many years. There seems to be one old man in particular, who may have been the miller. Anyway, he doesn't seem to bother anyone, but the building is kept locked now so that the curious can't get in and look."

"We can't go in?" another tourist asked.

"No, I'm afraid not. All right, let's move on. I want to show you the church and the bell tower."

The group moved on, but Stefano gobbled down his sandwich and rushed to Vincenzo's house. Since his friend lived six streets from the piazza, he was out of breath when Vincenzo opened the door.

"Guess what! Guess what!" he managed to get out.

"What?"

"That old…that old…building next to our house?"

"*Vecchio Mulino*?"

"The old mill, yes."

"What about it?"

"It's…it's haunted!"

"Come on."

Vincenzo closed the door and sat on the doorstep with Stefano next to him.

"It's true," Stefano said. "There was this tourist lady leading a bunch of people, I think they were from Germany or maybe France but they spoke Italian so I understood."

"Any they said?"

"The tourist lady told them that there were hundreds of ghosts in there!"

"Come on, Stefano."

"She said it! And she said there was a ghost of an old man in there and every night he would come out and scare people. Really scare people! It's true!"

"Stefano, how many times have we walked past that building? We've never seen a ghost, have we?"

"Well, no…"

"And you've never seen an old man ghost at night, right?"

"I guess…"

"So there aren't any ghosts there. Anyway, I don't believe in ghosts. You don't, do you?"

"Um, no. Of course not. I don't believe in ghosts. That's stupid."

"Come on, let's play soccer."

After an hour of something less than hard-fought soccer, Stefano went home. But not before circling *Vecchio Mulino.* He went up the stairs on the outside, past the grinding wheel, and he looked in the windows. No one had lived in the building for years, and Stefano could see only old machinery covered with dust. He crawled under the steps and tried in vain to open the thick wooden door. He knocked loudly but actually hoped no one would answer. No one did.

At dinner that night, he brought up the question. Did they believe in ghosts? Papa and Mama replied vaguely. They themselves had never seen a ghost next door, but the family had been here for only a few months.

Nonno was silent, but after dinner, he settled into his big chair and picked up the half-finished reed basket he'd been making.

"Do you believe in ghosts, Grandfather?"

"You know, Stefano, Italians seem to love ghosts and witches and all sorts of supernatural things. I don't know why, nobody does. Maybe they like to be in touch with another world. Maybe they like to be scared. Anyway, it's all part of our heritage."

"I don't believe in ghosts or witches."

"Stefano, you believed in *La Befana* for years. And she's a witch."

"I don't any more. I know that Papa and Mama leave me Christmas presents, not some stupid old witch. Only little kids believe in *La Befana.*"

Nonno threaded another strip into the basket. "Not only children believe. There's a village in the Abruzzo, Castel del Monte, where there's a legend that when children got sick it was because witches entered through a keyhole and sucked their blood."

"Come on."

"Even now, every year, the people of the village have a *La Notte delle Streghe*, Night of the Witches, and they wear witches' costumes and light candles and have a banquet."

"I don't believe in witches."

"How about ghosts? Tuscany is filled with ghosts. They say that Napoleon's ghost has been seen in Lucca because he got mad when they put up a statue of somebody else instead of him. And there was a beautiful woman in Lucca called Lucida Mansi who sold her soul to the devil in exchange for another thirty years of youth. When the thirty years were up she changed her mind but the devil pursued her. She fled in a carriage which ended up in the botanical gardens and you can still see her face there. Or so they say."

"They say stupid things."

"And there's supposed to be a witches' coven on Mount Matanna in the Garfagnana where a ghost with a scythe guards a golden treasure.

"And there's the famous story of the beautiful Donna Bianca in Fiesole who died of a broken heart when her husband was killed on their wedding day. She haunts a castle there in her wedding dress.

"Also, there's a church near Siena where you can hear a chorus of drunken people sing at night because that's what they were doing when the floor opened up and they fell into flames. And a palazzo in Florence that always keeps a window open where a young bride awaits her husband's return from war."

Stefano stood up, stretched his legs and sat down again. "OK. OK. I don't believe in ghosts."

"How about devils?"

"Devils?"

"Devils are all over Tuscany, too. In fact, there's a *Valle del Diavolo*, or the Devil's Valley, which is supposed to have inspired Dante's *Inferno*. It's an area near Lardarello southwest of Florence that is known for its huge eruptions of steam and sulfur. Yes, it smells."

"Yuck."

"Also, remember when we went to Pisa and saw the leaning tower?"

"Papa and me climbed to the top!"

"Remember we also went to the cathedral nearby?"

"Sort of."

"Well, I didn't show you then, but there's a piece of marble on the north façade that has many many small holes and there's a story about that. It seems that when the cathedral was being built, the devil was jealous, and he climbed on the roof to stop it. But an angel frightened him and the only thing he could do was cling to the piece of marble with his nails. So that's why there are holes."

"Oh, come on."

"But my favorite devil's story is at Borgo e Mozzano. Remember when we went to the factory that makes those delicate figures in our *presepio?*"

"Yes! Yes! We saw them make the boy with the flute! And the woman with the geese! All those people."

"Well, remember we also saw that beautiful bridge near the village?"

"The one that's has a big hump in the middle."

"That's called a humpback bridge. But it's known around there as the Devil's Bridge."

"I bet because he built it, right?"

"Well, its real name is the *Ponte della Maddalena* because there was once a statue of Mary Magdalene at one end. But nobody calls it that. It's *Ponte del Diavolo*. And it's become a famous story."

"And you're going to tell me."

"Sometime in the Middle Ages, a master builder was contracted to construct a new bridge across the Serchio, which winds its way through the Garfagnana."

"And comes near here."

"The builder's work went slowly until he realized he couldn't make the deadline the villagers had given him. He was desperate.

"Suddenly, a tall, well-dressed merchant stood next to him. The man told the builder that he could finish the bridge that night, but there was one condition. The builder must give him the soul of the first living thing that crossed the bridge when it was completed. The builder agreed, and the next day the villagers had their beautiful bridge."

"I think there's a catch coming."

"When they congratulated the builder," Nonno continued, "he told them that no one should cross the bridge until sunset. The builder then rode his horse to Lucca to seek the bishop's advice."

"And the bishop said?"

"Fool the devil, the wise bishop said. Send a pig across first."

"A pig?"

"The builder found a pig and let it cross. The devil was so furious that he had been tricked that he threw himself into the Serchio."

"Good story!" Stefano said. "But I don't believe it."

"Sometimes, the story changes, and it's a goat or a donkey that's sent across. Also, I read that there are nine devil's bridges in Italy alone and maybe up to two dozen in Europe."

"I guess the devil must have been very busy."

Nonno put the basket down. He'd completed two more rows. "That's enough for tonight," he said.

Stefano got up. "So what do all these stories about witches and ghosts and devils have to do with the ghost next door? Not that I believe that there's a ghost next door."

Nonno thought for a moment. "Stefano, as you grow older, I think you will appreciate the many legends that Italy has. They may not all be true—in fact, many aren't. But they are stories handed down from generation to generation, and they make us realize what a fanciful heritage we have. We can believe them or not, whatever we choose."

Stefano was on his way upstairs when he turned around. "Nonno, do you believe there's a ghost next door?"

"All I can say is I that I haven't seen one—yet."

CHIESA DI SANTA ZITA

CHIESA DI SANTA ZITA

STEFANO NEVER LIKED going to Mass when they lived in San Domenico. The church was cold and damp even in summer, and the service lasted forever. There were dozens of statues and paintings and candles all over the place, and the old priest had a long white beard that made him look like one of the Old Testament prophets in the stained glass windows. Worse, he said the Mass in Latin even after the pope said it was fine to say it in Italian.

Stefano squirmed through much of the Mass, avoiding his mother's stern gaze and his father's heavy hand on his knee.

The small church in San Ferdinando was different. There was a statue above the door and three tall windows over that. Inside, it was largely unadorned: A simple altar under a large crucifix, small shrines on either side, two banks of candles at the entrance. The one exception was a side altar with the statue of a young woman. She was dressed in black, wore a white apron and carried a basket of what appeared to be bread. The red votive candles in front of her were always lit.

"That's Saint Zita," Nonno informed Stefano after they'd been in San Ferdinando for a few weeks. They were eating their ice cream cones on the bench opposite the church.

"Who was she?"

"Well," said Nonno, licking a drip from his cone, "remember when we went to the Church of San Frediano in Lucca?"

"The white one with the mural on top?"

"That's the one. Remember anything else about it?"

"Um…um…oh, I remember! Yuck!"

"Why yuck?"

"The body. There's a body under an altar! Yuck."

"And that's Saint Zita."

"Herself? Really?"

"Really. When they dug up her body years ago they found that it had not decayed, so they mummified it and put it under the altar."

"I didn't even want to look at it. Why did they dig it up in the first place?"

"They were starting the process of making Zita a saint. It took a long time, but she was made a saint in the Seventeenth century. She was born late in the Thirteenth century. I used to know the dates, but I can't remember dates any more. I guess I'm getting old."

"You're not getting old, Nonno. You remember everything!"

"I wish I did." He took off his cap and wiped his forehead. "Anyway, let me tell you something about Saint Zita."

As they looked at the church, the old man recounted how Zita was born not far away, in Monsagratti, and as a girl went to work as a maid in the household of the Fatinelli family in Lucca.

"In fact, she prayed at the Church of San Frediano, where her body lies today."

"But she worked as a maid?"

"She cooked, she sewed, she cleaned, she did everything. And everything without a complaint. And she did all this after she had been up for hours praying and going to Mass at the Church of San Frediano. Of course, the other servants were jealous and they tried to make her life miserable. But then some strange things happened."

"What?"

"One time, during a famine, she wanted to help poor people so she distributed beans from the kitchen."

"Just beans?"

"Well, that's the legend. Anyway, Signor Fatinelli was upset, but then it turned out that the bin of beans never got empty."

"A miracle!"

"Another time, on Christmas eve, she wanted to go to midnight Mass but it was freezing cold. Signor Fatinelli told her not to go, but she insisted. So he told her to wear a fur cloak that belonged to his wife. When she got to the Church of San Frediano she noticed a beggar who was crying. When he touched her fur coat she took it off and gave it to him."

"Wasn't she cold?"

"Yes, she was, and after the Mass she looked around but the beggar had disappeared. When she got home, Signor Fatinelli was upset that she'd given the beautiful cloak away but suddenly the beggar appeared and returned the cloak. And then he disappeared."

"Miracle two."

Stefano was getting into this now.

"Let me think," Nonno said. "I'm sure there are others. Oh yes. One time, she went outside the walls of Lucca to attend Mass and it was very late when she got back and the gates were locked. But then the Blessed Mother appeared, and the gates miraculously opened."

"Number three!"

"But the next miracle is probably the one people most remember. One morning, she started baking bread and was called away to help a poor family. When the other servants went into the kitchen, they saw a group of angels taking bread out of the ovens. They had finished the baking."

"Four!"

"And now she's the patron of maids. That's why her statue in the church has her wearing an apron and carrying bread."

"You told that well, Signor!"

Stefano and Nonno looked around. Father Antonio, the parish priest, was suddenly behind them, a cup of coffee in one hand and a sweet roll in the other.

"Sorry, but I've been listening to your story, Signor. I hope you don't mind."

"Did I get it right?"

"Well, you know how stories change over the centuries. But, yes, there was a Saint Zita and she did work miracles. It's nice to have those stories, isn't it?"

Nonno and Stefano agreed.

Stefano always blushed when he saw the priest, who was so unlike the one in San Domenico. Father Antonio, or Tony as he liked to be called, had been ordained only ten years ago. He had black curly hair, a stubble of a beard and bright blue eyes. Often, he didn't even wear his Roman collar when he went out on the piazza, and he enjoyed playing checkers with the elderly men in front of the *Trattoria*. He helped the Ladies of Charity with their spaghetti dinners and played the victim at water-dunking games.

He organized soccer teams for both boys and girls, and both Stefano and Vincenzo were on the boys' teams. Sometimes he rented a bus to take kids, accompanied by a few parents, to Florence to see the magnificent art works, or, better yet, to the beaches at Pietrasanta.

"God is everywhere," he would say. "We just have to find Him."

Finishing his sweet roll, the priest stood up.

"Are you looking forward to the festival, Stefano?"

"What festival?"

"The one that honors Santa Zita."

THE BELL TOWER

GUELPHS AND GHIBELLINES

SINCE THE CHURCH was so close, Stefano was used to hearing the bells from the nearby tower. When they rang at 6 a.m. he turned over and went back to sleep, snuggling with Enrico. When it was noon, he went and helped the bell ringer, an elderly man with a scruffy beard, pull the rope. At 6 p.m., just before supper, he looked out the window and counted: three times, three times, three times, nine times. Satisfied that the bell ringer got it right, he went down to eat.

"He always gets it right," he thought. "That's no fun."

One night, Nonno thought that if Stefano heard a story about the bell tower he would appreciate it more. Working on a round basket with a handle, he called the boy to his side.

"Ready for another story?"

"Always."

"First, I need to give you some background. In the Middle Ages, the central part of Italy, including this area, was pretty much divided in two. One part was controlled by the pope, who was very powerful then. He even had his own army. But there was also an emperor who opposed the pope and he had his own army. So the two armies fought each other, over and over again, to get more territory. The people who supported the pope were called the Guelphs…"

"The dwarfs?"

"No, the Guelphs. Guelphs. And then there were the armies who supported the emperor. They were called the Ghibellines."

"I'm not even going to try to say that name."

"Well, the Guelphs often came from wealthy families who made their money in the mercantile trade. The Ghibellines were also wealthy, but their money generally came from huge agricultural estates.

"Smaller cities tended to be Ghibelline if the larger city nearby was Guelph. For example, Pisa and Siena and Lucca tended to be Ghibelline because Florence was Guelph. In fact, the most famous battle of the Middle Ages, one that you should look up in your book, was fought at a town called Montaperti in 1260. It was between the Florentines, who you remember were Guelph, and the Siennese, who you remember were Ghibelline.

"Well, the army from Siena was vastly outnumbered, but they still routed the Florentines. In fact, it was the worst battle ever in the Middle Ages and Dante even wrote about it in the *Inferno*. Some 10,000 men were killed on the Guelph side with 4,000 missing and 15,000 captured. Only 600 Ghibelline soldiers died."

"Wow, Nonno. That's amazing. That's like two to one! Or three to one! Four to one. I don't know. Anyway, the Gizziline soldiers won big."

"Ghibelline."

"Right. So how was the village of San Ferdinando involved in all this?"

"San Ferdinando, like Pisa and Siena, was Ghibelline, had been for many years. They mainly fought with Lucca, but sometimes there were smaller skirmishes between San Ferdinando and another village that was Guelph. One would invade the other and one side would win and then the other side would invade, and that side would win, and on and on."

"Sounds kind of boring."

"Not if you were in one of the villages and the enemy showed up at your door."

"Bummer!"

"And that's what happened here about a hundred years before the battle of Montaperti. San Ferdinando was much smaller then. The piazza was only just started. The church was here, and the bell tower. The building that's now the *Pizzeria* was there, and the *Albergo*. And the one where the *Profumeria* is. That small tower over there. A couple of other buildings were here then, but eventually they were torn down. There were a few houses outside the piazza but mostly it was farmland.

"Here's another difference. If you think about the armies that fought at Montaperti you probably think that they were all decked out in bright shiny armor and silver helmets and they carried long spears and bows and arrows, and their horses wore all kinds of armor, too."

Stefano got excited. "Yes! There are pictures in my medieval book of the mesh armor they put on first, then the metal armor on top of that, and then the helmets and shields and the swords and the crossbows! I wish I had a crossbow."

Nonno was almost finished with his new basket and began preparing the strip that would form the handle.

"That might have been the case for the armies in the big cities, but not for the little towns like San Ferdinando. Here, they were lucky if they had a decent shield. Mostly they wore brown tunics and leggings and sometimes a heavy cap. The Guelph armies wore a big patch of red cloth on their chests to show their loyalty to the pope, and the Ghibelline armies wore blue because they were loyal to the emperor. Really, both were pretty much ragtag outfits."

"OK, what about the battle here, in San Ferdinando?"

"Well, as I said, this was a Ghibelline town and they had an army of, at most, twenty or twenty-five men. The problem was they had gone without a battle for a long time, months, and were getting lazy. And they weren't paying much attention to the Guelphs, even though they knew Guelph soldiers were hiding in the forests in the hills outside of here."

"You mean those forests over there?"

"Yes. They were even thicker then. Well, one night, the soldiers here were enjoying the beer and ale that several of them had made. They were in the house where the *Pizzeria* is now. They were very drunk and most of them fell asleep. They were laying on the floor, on benches. One of them hung out the window."

Stefano began to laugh.

"They were making so much noise that the Guelphs in the hills heard them. Two of them, teenagers who were twins, Antonio and Amadeo, volunteered to go down to the village to see what was going on. So they crept down and came into the piazza right over there, next to the bell tower.

"It didn't take long for them to find the drunken soldiers. So they knew they had to get word to their companions in the hills. There was an obvious way to do that. They went into the bell tower and rang the bell. Over and over. One of the local soldiers finally work up. 'What's happening?' he said."

"Well," Stefano shouted. "I know what was happening. The church bells are ringing and the Dwarfs are coming! The Dwarfs are coming! Wake up!"

"Well, it didn't take long before all the Guelph soldiers, even though there were only about twenty of them, descended on the town, went into that house, and woke up the drunken Ghibellines. The Guelphs wanted to capture the Ghibellines, but one of the Ghibellines said, 'Wouldn't you like to have a drink with us?' They didn't even realize that they were talking to the enemy."

"Didn't they notice that the dwarfs were wearing red?"

"They were too drunk. So Amadeo looked at Antonio and Antonio looked at Amadeo and they shrugged and said, 'OK.' And soon all the Guelphs were drinking and telling jokes and the Ghibellines were telling jokes. And they had too much to drink. By morning, they had all fallen asleep, the Guelphs and the Ghibellines were falling all over each other.

"When they all woke up, they wondered why they were fighting in the first place. Antonio and Amadeo looked at each other and suggested that they should have a party. They would invite not only the people in San Ferdinando but also the people from the farms and hills around there. And you know how they invited them?"

"They rang the church bells!"

"Of course. And they had their party, which lasted almost a week, and for all the time after that no one thought of themselves as a Guelph or a Ghibelline, but just someone who lived in San Ferdinando."

"Nonno, now I know you make these stories up."

"Stefano, someday you'll tell these stories to your grandson."

THE *PROFUMERIA*

THE *CONTRADE*

RAIN HAD DRENCHED all the hills and villages in the area overnight, and the field where Stefano and Vincenzo played soccer was filled with puddles. Vincenzo had come over anyway, and the boys were, as Stefano's mother said, beside themselves. Since Papa had to go to school for a meeting, she and Nonno were left alone with them.

"Why don't you play chess?" she suggested.

That lasted less than an hour before Stefano accused Vincenzo of cheating and Vincenzo accused Stefano of cheating and Stefano threw the king across the room and Vincenzo upset the entire board.

"OK," Stefano's mother said, "you can play your videogames but, remember, only for an hour."

They stretched that past the limit and then lay on the floor, sulking. Nonno saw that his daughter was almost in tears as she rolled out the dough for the ravioli they would have on Sunday.

"I know," he said to the boys, "let's go for a walk. It's stopped raining, and there's a place I want to show you."

Outside, only a few people were in the piazza, carefully picking their way around the puddles between the cobblestones. Shopkeepers were raising the steel gates to their stores, and four elderly men were setting up a table to play *scopa*. Father Antonio emerged from the church and crossed the piazza to get coffee. The two resident cats were still chasing each other around the well.

"Follow me," Nonno said as he led the boys to a tall stone building of varying heights with a large archway in the middle. A sign on one part said *Profumeria*.

"What's a *profumeria*?" Stefano asked.

"It's a place that sells perfumes and cosmetics. Your father always buys your mother a Christmas present here."

"My father, too," Vincenzo said. "The same thing every year. A bottle of perfume. It's because he can't think of anything else to buy her. She always smiles and says thanks but I know she'd rather get a gift card to a store in Lucca. She even told me."

"It may be a perfume store now," Nonno said, "but in the Middle Ages it was something much more exciting. Come."

They entered the building by a short flight of steps to the left of the shop, then up a long flight of stairs to the second floor.

"Wow!" Stefano and Vincenzo said together.

In a space that spread through half the floor, they could see dozens and dozens of brightly colored flags, some small, some large, many of them hung from the ceiling and some encased in glass on the walls. A tiny man with a large humpback shuffled toward them.

"*Buongiorno,* Franco," Nonno said.

"*Buongiorno,* Emilio," the man said. "*Benvenuto!*"

It was one of the rare times that Stefano had heard his grandfather called by his real name.

"*Come stai,* Franco?" Nonno asked.

Franco embarked on a long story of the pains in his legs, his back, his arms, his feet, and then went into his frequent stomach aches and his terrible headaches and ended with "*Buono.* I'm good."

Nonno explained to Franco that he wanted his grandson and his friend to see this beautiful display and to hear the history of the place.

"*Buono! Buono!*" Franco said. "Sit, sit, sit. Would the boys like a snack?"

The boys would.

Franco went to a small refrigerator in the corner and returned with two cans of Coke and a small plate of *biscotti.* Each boy took two.

The two old men settled on a sunken couch at the end of the room and the boys sat opposite them on folding chairs, their feet dangling as they munched their cookies. Nonno took out his pipe.

"You begin," Franco said.

"Stefano," Nonno began, "remember when I told you that San Ferdinando, as with many small villages, liked to mimic their big neighbors, for example setting up a *calcio storico* the same as Florence."

"I remember that. The bloody fight."

"Siena, though, was a model for something else. In the Middle Ages, the city was separated into districts that were set up to supply armies that defended the city from Florence and other nearby city states. The districts were called *contrade* and there were seventeen of them."

"And they each had a name," Franco said. "There was the *Contrada del Bruco,* or Caterpillar, the *Contrada dell'Aquila,* or Eagle, the *Contrada del Drago,* or Dragon…"

"The *Contrada della Giraffa,* the Giraffe," Nonno added. "The *Contrada dell'Oca,* the Goose…"

"The Goose!" Vincenzo shouted. He and Stefano almost fell off their chairs. Their elders ignored them.

"People who don't live in Siena can't understand this," Franco said, "but the *contrada* gives each person who lives there, well, an identity. It's still true today. They don't say they live in Siena. They say they live in *Contrada del Drago* or *Contrada della Giraffa…*"

"Or the Goose!" Stefano shouted.

"Settle down, Stefano," Nonno said. "To this day in Siena, every *contrada* has its own customs, its history and its celebrations. They each have their own church where they celebrate baptisms, deaths, marriages. They have their own dinners and festivals."

"And," Franco said, "they are very competitive, often getting into fights with someone from another *contrada.*" Stefano and Vincenzo grew more interested.

"OK," Nonno said. "That's Siena. Now let's talk about San Ferdinando. As I said, this village likes to copy, so way back in the Middle Ages, it set up *contrade,* too. But because it was so small, there were only four of them, the *Contrada della Pantera,* or Panther, the *Contrada della Tartaruga,* or Tortoise, the *Contrada della Selva,* or Forest, and the *Contrada della Torre,* or Tower."

"That's the *contrada* where we are now," Franco said.

"No goose?" Stefano asked.

Ignoring him, Nonno continued. "Each of them had a banner and a headquarters on the piazza and its residents lived just behind it."

Franco added, "What a time that was. There was such spirit in each of the *contrade.* Everyone helped one another! And the parties! They set up tables on the piazza in front of their headquarters and they ate and drank into the night."

Stefano and Vincenzo saw that Franco had tears in his eyes.

"And there even was a song. It was borrowed from the Tower *contrada* in Siena."

"I remember hearing that long ago," Nonno said. "Do you still remember it?"

Franco thought a bit, and then, in a high throaty voice, he began to sing.

A te va la gloria
con te la vittoria
perchè solo tu
sai l'onor conquistar

Beltà nel vessillo
che in ciel sventolerà:
sarà, sarà la Torre
che trionferà!

Nonno and the boys applauded, and Franco really did start crying. He took out a red handkerchief and blew his nose.

"What did that mean, Nonno?" Stefano asked.

"Well, let me try," he said, and in a deep throaty voice he began.

Glory is yours
victory with you
because only you
know the honor to win.

Beauty in the banner
that in heaven will fly:
Will be the Tower
that will triumph!

The boys applauded again, and Franco joined in.

Nonno put down his pipe. "Well, Franco, should we tell the boys about the *palio*?"

"Why not."

Nonno explained that in Siena, twice each summer, a famous horse race is run around their piazza, which is called the Campo there. The place is filled with dirt and before the race there is a long parade and the men wear medieval costumes and there are bugles and drums.

Franco smiled in agreement, and Nonno continued.

"There are ten horses representing the seventeen *contrade* because seventeen would be too many to race. The horse is like a saint. They even bring it to their church to be blessed beforehand."

"Come on!" both boys said.

"They do!" Franco said. "And the priest tells each one of them to be victorious."

"How can they all be victorious?" Vincenzo asked. "Isn't there only one winner?"

"Of course," the old man said. "It's just what he says."

Nonno continued. "The race only takes about a minute and a half and it's the most exciting thing. People come from all over to watch, and the *contrada* that has the winning horse goes crazy. You can see this on YouTube. It's like the world championship of every sport rolled into one. The celebrations go on for days."

"Can we go, Nonno? Can we go?"

"Me, too!" Vincenzo said.

"Maybe someday when you're older. You'll have to ask your Mama and Papa."

"Well," Franco said, "San Ferdinando copied the race, starting in the Seventeenth century. The *Palio di San Ferdinando*! It was only once a year, always on the third Saturday in July so it wouldn't compete with Siena. They covered this piazza with sand. They trained horses in a field outside of town, and they had parades and parties beforehand. There was a lot of flag throwing and lots of singing. Then on the day of the palio, each *contrada* brought its horse to the church over there, and the priest blessed them."

The boys giggled.

"The race was pretty good," Nonno said, "but it was short, only about five minutes."

"Did you see that empty space near the steps when you came up?" Franco asked. "That's where the horse from the Tower *contrada* made its entrance."

Stefano and Vincenzo went to the window to look down on the space.

"Unfortunately," Franco said, "the palio stopped in San Ferdinando in 1951. The same horse had won four times in a row and a lot of cheating was suspected. Well, more than cheating. Bribes. Big bribes. There were accusations and fights and brawls and the Panther was fighting the Forest and the Tortoise was fighting everybody. Finally, people decided not to do it anymore."

Franco blew his nose before continuing.

"The headquarters of the other three *contrade* were in pretty bad shape. and they were torn down. But this one was good. We used to have the whole building. There was a dining hall where the *Profumeria* is now, and offices upstairs. This has always been the little museum and I'm the caretaker. Nobody comes to see it anymore, though. The last person was an old man from Perugia who came over Easter."

No one spoke for a while, and even the boys stopped fidgeting.

"We should be going," Nonno said, "but we would like a little tour of the museum if you don't mind."

"Of course! Of course! Let me show you."

Franco told them they were in a room called the Hall of Victories because it contained all the dozens of silk banners that the Tower *contrada's* horses had won over the centuries. Because they were so old, many were encased in glass and hung on the walls.

"These are called *drappelloni*," he said. "They were paraded around the streets after the races. Every one of them has a depiction of the Virgin Mary, because the races were dedicated to her. You see many are so old they are frayed and faded."

Stefano and Vincenzo walked around the room looking at the dates, which were in order. "1694!" "1703!" "1718!" and on and on. The last was in 1947.

"Wow!" they said together.

"And these banners," Franco said as they moved on, "were awarded for best representing their *contrada* in the parades before the races."

The older ones were behind glass but the ones from the last century hung in rows from the ceiling.

"Wow!"

Moving to another room, Franco explained that they were entering "The Hall of History." On display, hanging on the walls and from the ceiling, in glass boxes and on pedestals, were suits of armor, helmets, tunics, doublets, jackets, hose, caps, capes, boots. All in bright colors and beautifully embroidered.

"Wow! Wow! Wow!"

The boys ran from one spot to another pointing and urging one another to "Come see this!" Nonno and Franco walked leisurely through. When they were finally able to drag the boys away, Franco led them to a small room that held ancient religious paintings and artifacts.

"Most of the important paintings are in Siena," he said, "but we are most proud of this one, a Crucifixion by Rutilio di Lorenzo Manetti from the Seventeenth century."

The boys could feel their eyes glaze over as they gazed at the rows of miters and stoles, cassocks and chasubles. They struggled to stay awake in front of the shelves of candlesticks and chalices. Nonno decided it was time to go home.

"How can we ever thank you, Franco! This has been a wonderful day. Look at the boys. They're in a daze. They'd never seen anything like this."

"Come back again," Franco said. "I'm glad you could see it. We don't get many visitors at this little museum anymore. The *Contrada della Torre* isn't like it was. People have friends all over the village now. They party together, they go to soccer games together. The other day I heard that a young man from the *Contrada dell'Aquila* was going to marry a girl from the *Contrada della Giraffa*. Can you imagine?"

"I wish I could have seen the palio," Stefano said.

Nonno and Franco exchanged glances and smiled.

"Wait until the the *Festa della Santa Zita di San Ferdinando*," Nonno said.

"Grandfather," Stefano said. "You're laughing again. Why?"

"You'll see."

THE *TRATTORIA*

ARLECCHINO

AS SOON AS HE SAW what was going on in the piazza, Stefano ran down the stairs and took his customary seat on the top step in front of the door. Husky men had just carried a coffin out of the Chiesa di Santa Zita and past a line of people waiting to go in and baptize a little girl. The baby was screaming and the mourners frowned. A television station in Florence had been alerted to this unusual juxtaposition of death and life, and a camera crew, scriptwriters and sound engineers began recording it for posterity. They, in turn, were chronicled by a bespectacled young reporter from *La Nazione* whose sweat was staining his new white shirt.

Shopkeepers came out to observe all this, and office workers stopped to listen. The old men took a break from playing *scopa,* and Franco looked out the window of the museum of the *Contrada della Torre.*

Things were going well until the baby let out a terrifying scream. One of the casket bearers lost his grip and the coffin dropped almost to the ground. The television director was aghast and tried to explain to the mourners that he couldn't air something like this and wanted them to start over. The mourners shouted, the baby's family yelled, and the onlookers cheered and applauded. The TV man began shouting, and the mourners and baptismal people yelled louder and the onlookers hooted and hollered. The reporter from *La Nazione* was taking notes furiously. Stefano was so excited he jumped up and down. Finally, Father Antonio emerged from the church and told the camera crew in no uncertain words where they could put their film.

Eventually, the camera crew fled, the funeral cortege made its way out through Porta Santa Maria and the baptismal family entered the church. Everyone else went back to work and Franco resumed polishing candlesticks in the museum.

Now bored, because Vincenzo had to go to the dentist that day, Stefano decided to take a tour of the piazza. He went in the back rooms of the the *Panetteria* and the *Gelateria* because he had only seen the front of the shops, and spent the longest time behind the *Trattoria.*

Over dinner that night, the boy regaled his family with the story of the happenings in the piazza. Most of it was factual, except for the part about the casket crashing to the ground and the body falling out.

"Don't make stuff up, Stefano," his father said.

"It's true! Sort of."

After dinner, while Papa did the dishes and Mama brought out her knitting, Nonno opened the book he was re-reading for the umpteenth time, *The Stories of Luigi Pirandello*. He had taken a break from making baskets.

Kneeling on the floor nearby, Stefano played a videogame for a while and then put down his joystick. "Nonno, can I ask you a question?"

"Of course."

"Today," Stefano said, "I went in back of the *Trattoria,* those rooms behind the shop."

"Stefano," his mother said, "you know you're not supposed to go back there. Isn't it locked?"

"No, it was open. And nobody was around so I went in. You should see what's back there! A whole bunch of chairs and tables, but the neat thing was this bunch of costumes. They looked like they were from the old, old days. Really bright. Why were they there?"

"I don't think I know," his mother said. "Maybe from a play long ago? Do you know, Father?"

Nonno finished reading a paragraph and put down his book.

"Close. I'm pretty sure they were from a group of actors called *Commedia dell'arte* who traveled all over Italy in medieval times. San Ferdinando was too small to have a theater, so the actors performed in the piazza. They came here often and they used that back area as dressing rooms, so they must have left their costumes there."

"There were a lot of them," Stefano said.

"And I'm sure they are beautiful. Now the *Commedia dell'arte* is something you should know about, Stefano, if you're going to have any knowledge of the Middle Ages."

Stefano settled back for another history lesson.

"*Commedia dell'arte,*" Nonno said, "is one of the great contributions Italy has made to all forms of entertainment. It began in Italy in the Sixteenth century and it became so popular that it spread throughout Europe way into the Eighteenth century."

"But what was it?"

"Basically they were little plays that were mostly improvised, and there was a lot of pantomime. The actors played stock characters, beautiful young women, foolish old men, devious servants. I remember there was one called *Il Dottore*, a doctor who knew everything. There was a greedy old man called Pantalone, and a servant girl named Colombina. And then there was Arlecchino. When *Commedia dell'arte* went to England, the British called him Harlequin. I think he's my favorite character."

"I know, I know!" Stefano exclaimed. "There was a poster of him there. Arle…somebody."

"Arlecchino always wore a colorful patchwork costume. He was a servant, but he often acted to foil the plans of his master because they were both in love with Colombina. But Colombina was faithless. She wouldn't love anybody. And so Arlecchino's heart was always broken."

"He looked very sad on the poster."

"There's a story about the actor who played the last Arlecchino here. I suppose you want to hear it?"

"Is it sad?

"Yes."

"Then, sure."

"His name was Luca di Lucca. He was from a small town outside of Lucca and he was with the troupe for many years. They played all over, cities like Pisa and Livorno but mostly small villages like San Ferdinando. He played *Il Dottore* a few times but then the actor who played Arlecchino got sick so Luca took over his part.

"On his third visit here he was resting after a performance when a young woman came up and offered him a glass of water. It was very warm and he was tired, so of course he accepted.

"The girl sat down and they began talking. He asked her a lot of questions but she didn't seem to want to talk about herself. She kept changing the subject and asked about him instead. He said he was from a farm, the youngest of seven children and had run away when he was sixteen because he hated taking care of pigs. He never wanted to see a pig again, he said.

"The girl asked him if he liked playing Arlecchino, and he said he did because then he could be somebody else. He didn't have to be a shy boy who fed pigs anymore but he could be a real man with real emotions.

"The girl didn't understand what he meant, but she said she would come to visit him again the next time the *Commedia dell'arte* troupe was in San Ferdinando.

"And she did. The troupe came every year, in July, and the girl, whose name was Micaela, visited him every time. And they talked and talked, and Micaela always asked him a lot of questions but she avoided his questions.

"Sometimes they went for walks and Luca talked about the other villages the troupe had visited. But as soon as it got dark Micaela said she had to go home. Luca said he would walk her home but Micaela said no, she wanted to walk by herself.

"After a couple of years, Luca told Micaela he was in love with her and wanted to marry her. He even got down on his knees and begged. He said he would quit the *Commedia dell'arte* troupe and live with her wherever she wanted.

"But then Micaela confessed that the very next month she was going to marry another man, a very rich man, because her father insisted. She didn't love him but her father said that she had to marry him.

"The next day, the troupe left San Ferdinando. When it came back the following year Luca was not a part of it. Somebody else was playing Arlecchino. Micaela asked the other actors where Luca was and they said he went back to his family farm to raise pigs."

The room was silent.

"That's it?" Stefano asked.

"I'm afraid so," Nonno said.

"Bummer."

"Well," Nonno said, "not all stories have happy endings."

PICCOLA TORRE

A ROYAL NEIGHBOR

OF ALL THE BUILDINGS in the piazza of San Ferdinando, the most curious was a tower next to Porta Santa Maria. Except for the *Trattoria,* it was the smallest building in the piazza, and it was dwarfed by a high tower next to it. People called it the *Piccola Torre,* the tiny tower.

Curiously, it was round, with only a single entrance and a lone window above it. On top of that was a room with a grate instead of a window, so Stefano guessed that must have been used as a prison.

And most unusual, late at night until early in the morning, a motorcycle rested near the door. Cars, motorcycles and bicycles were banned from the piazza, but since the building was only feet from the gate, everyone presumed it was allowed.

For once, Nonno did not have many answers when Stefano asked him about the building. It was indeed a prison, or *prigione,* in the Middle Ages, he said, and was used by the Ghibellines to hold the Guelphs that they captured.

"Why was it so small?" Stefano asked.

"Well, remember that San Ferdinando was small and didn't have much of any army. Neither did the Guelphs. So they didn't need a big prison. And the Ghibellines usually let their prisoners go free after a while. When it comes down it it, they really didn't like to fight."

Nonno said he didn't know much else about the building.

"Grandfather, why is that motorcycle there sometimes?"

"I've asked about that, too. Somebody said the man who lives there works in Lucca, so it's usually there only at night. Nobody seems to know much about him or what he does."

Stefano kept an eye on the building every time he walked past, but never saw a sign of life. That is, until one night when he was in the middle of his *Donkey Kong* game and he heard terrible screeching outside.

"It's Enrico! He must have gotten out!"

Darting out the door, Stefano traced the shrieking sounds to *Piccola Torre.* Enrico, his back arched and his eyes glowing, was shaking and rumbling a few feet from the steps. Stefano saw that he was about to attack a small white cat on the doorstep. Its back was also arched and it was clearly terrified.

"No, Enrico, no!"

Enrico yowled some more.

"No, Enrico! Come here!"

Enrico growled and the white cat tried to back into the door.

"No! I've got you!"

Stefano grabbed Enrico just as it was about to pounce and held the struggling cat in his arms. The door suddenly opened. "Hey! What's all this noise about?"

The man picked up the white cat and held it close. He was about forty years old, big and burly, with black hair in a ponytail and a beard that hadn't been shaved in several days. He wore a plaid flannel shirt, black pants and heavy work shoes.

"It's nothing, Sir." Stefano was so scared he could barely speak. "My cat was just teasing your cat."

"What's your cat's name?"

"Enrico, Sir."

"That's a nice name. My cat here is Sweetie."

"Sweetie?"

"Yes."

The man held his cat out, and Stefano reached out with one hand to pet it while holding Enrico tightly under his other arm. Sweetie purred.

"She likes you," the man said.

Sweetie purred some more.

"She really likes you."

They sat on the step, the big man petting the little Sweetie and small Stefano scratching the struggling Enrico's ears. Stefano said he lived next door with his parents and grandfather and that they had moved from another village a couple of months ago.

The man asked Stefano if he liked cats and the boy of course replied that he loved them, that Enrico was his favorite thing in the whole world.

After a while the man had an idea.

"Say, you know I work all day and I leave some food out for Sweetie but I know she gets lonesome. I wonder if you'd like to come over and play with her once in a while. Would you like that?"

"Would I? Really?"

"I could pay you a little."

"No, no. Really?"

"Sure. Why don't you have your parents come over and we can talk about it."

Mama and Papa and Nonno were playing three-hand *briscola* when Stefano returned with Enrico still tussling in his arms.

"Where have you been?" Papa asked. "We were about to call the *polizia*."

Stefano caught his breath and proceeded to tell the amazing story of how Enrico had saved a teeny tiny little white cat from some horrible disaster.

"Where was this?" Mama asked.

"At that little tower."

"Was the man home?"

"Yes. And guess what? He wants me to come over and play with his cat sometime. He wants you to go over and talk to him about it. Oh, and the cat's name is Sweetie."

"Sweetie?" Papa, Mama and Nonno said together.

"What's the man's name?" Papa asked.

"Um, I guess I didn't get that."

"Right."

The family went to the tower after the *passeggiata* the next time they saw that the motorcycle was outside.

The place was even smaller than they had imagined. There was only one small round room, furnished with a table, two chairs, a cot, a sink and a microwave. The visitors presumed a space behind a curtain was a makeshift bathroom.

Despite the modest conditions, the room was painted a bright yellow and bathed in light from the window even at this hour. Under the window was a banner containing a coat of arms.

Stefano sat on one of the chairs and was immediately pulled up by his father. "Let your mother and Nonno sit," he said.

The others stood, almost shoulder to shoulder. Sweetie observed them warily from a shelf near the ceiling.

"I'm sorry," the man said. "I should have introduced myself. I'm Carlo Roberto."

Papa, Mama and Nonno introduced themselves, and hands were shaken all around. While the others made light conversation, Nonno couldn't take his eyes off the banner.

"Carlo Roberto," he said, "I've been looking at that beautiful banner you have there."

"Oh yes. It's been in the family for generations, well, even longer. You can see that there are rips and it's getting pretty faded, but I like the colors and what it means to me so I keep it there."

"But," Nonno said, "I notice the symbols that are on it. The shield, the arrow, the lion, the book. Could this be the banner of Duke Carlo, the first ruler of San Ferdinando? Didn't he have it made in the 1500s?"

"I'm afraid so," Carlo Roberto said.

"So you are?"

"Yes, one of the many many descendants of Duke Carlo and Lucia. We're scattered all over now. I don't even know where most of them are. I exchange emails with a distant cousin in Germany at Christmas, but that's about the only connection I have. It's kind of sad actually. I wish we had kept things up and that somebody had figured out a family tree. But it's too late now."

"But you have the banner," Papa said.

"Yes. Somebody was going to throw it away but my father rescued it."

Nonno turned to his grandson. "Stefano, remember when I told you about the first ruler of San Ferdinando?"

"Um, sort of."

"Well, I did. And that his name was Carlo and his wife was Lucia and his son was Roberto…"

"And," Stefano interrupted, "Carlo didn't want Roberto to marry some girl but he did anyway and they had lots of children but nobody knows where they are."

"Well, here's one of them. This man, this man who has Sweetie the cat, is one of his many descendants."

"Really? Really? Wow!"

There were now so many questions that everyone was talking at once. When things settled down, it was determined that, even though Carlo Roberto was of royal heritage, he was not at all wealthy. He had to work for a living. He had tried everything from teaching Italian in Japan to serving as a chef on a Saudi prince's yacht. "There were so many fights in the kitchen that I had to leave." He had had several love affairs but had never married. "Almost, one time. But she married somebody else."

He had, he said, never found any kind of fulfillment until now.

The others waited to hear more.

"I heard of this shelter for the homeless in Lucca," he said. "*San Francesco Casa per i Poveri.* Actually, it's more than a shelter, though it does have thirty beds. It serves supper every night, it provides clothing and even has computer classes. It's operated by the Capuchins and they were looking for someone to run the day-to-day operations. So I moved here and I foolishly applied and they foolishly accepted. It's a wonderful job. I couldn't be happier."

"That's amazing!"

"How good you must feel!"

"I imagine you don't get paid much."

"True," Carlo Roberto said. "I get a small stipend, but I get to eat with the clients. I don't need money. The motorcycle doesn't need much. I got this place for a song. Who else would want to live in a one-room round tower with a prison on top? There are disadvantages, yes. I work such long hours I'm rarely here so I haven't met many people in San Ferdinando. I'm sorry about that."

Mama gave Carlo Roberto a little hug. "Well, you've met us, and I hope we can be your friends. Always."

Finding that there were genial feelings between her master and the newcomers, Sweetie hopped down from her shelf and rubbed against Stefano's legs.

"And I can be friends with Sweetie," Stefano said. "Should I bring Enrico over to play?"

"No, better not."

THE *PANETTERIA*

VERONICA AND THE TROUBADOUR

MOST EVENINGS, Nonno enjoyed a *gelato* with Stefano after their *passeggiata* in the piazza. On Thursdays, however, they went next door to the *Panetteria* where he purchased an apricot *cornetto*.

"Nonno, why do you always go the *Panetteria* instead of the *Gelateria* on Thursdays?" Stefano asked.

"No reason, just a change of pace," his grandfather replied.

"And why do you always have a *cornetto* instead of a *gelato*?"

"Your Mama is always saying I should vary my diet."

"Nonno!"

"Stefano, at my age, one gets into a routine, and it's very hard to change. Anyway, I like to go to the *Panetteria* because it reminds me of a story. A sad story, but with a happy ending. Sort of."

"And you're going to tell me, right?"

Stefano got a *cornetto*, too, and they sat on their bench and watched as the remaining adults bought treats at the *Pasticceria* and *Galateria* and teenagers descended on the *Pizzeria*. The moon was just starting to rise above the bell tower next to the church, and people pulled on sweaters as the night got cooler.

Across the way, the *Panetteria* was surely one of the most beautiful buildings in the piazza. Three stories tall, it had well-maintained red tile roofs, flower boxes under its windows, and an arched doorway. The ground floor windows had been remodeled to showcase the long loaves of bread made inside, but one could imagine when they had opened to an opulent interior.

"I bet some rich people lived there," Stefano said.

"Very rich. The Cappellis were one of the wealthiest families in this whole part of Tuscany. They were a merchant family and made their money importing goods from China and the Far East, mostly by boat but sometimes on the Silk Road. But they were benevolent, and gave much to the Church and to organizations that helped the poor.

"One thing they did not have, though, was a line of descendants. The last Cappelli family that lived there had only a daughter, Veronica. She was a lovely child, happy, with many friends. Naturally, they doted on her and wanted her to have the best education before they could find a suitable husband for her. There were no good schools here, of course, so they sent her to Bologna, which, as you know, has the oldest university in the world. Girls couldn't attend classes, but they hired a private tutor who taught her how to read and write. This was almost unheard of then.

"She lived in a very nice apartment with a maid, and soon she began to explore the city. From what we know, student life was very active there then, and she became acquainted with some of the students. Particularly one."

"Oh, oh," Stefano said. "I know what's going to happen next."

"Yes. He was a handsome lad, a poet by the name of Pino who was trying to make a living as a troubadour. There weren't many in Italy, and his songs were in Latin, so he mainly sang at church events."

"And was poor!" Stefano said.

"Very. But he loved Veronica, and Veronica fell deeply in love with him. She left her maid behind and they snuck off to his room in the students' quarter. They enjoyed walking under the famous porticos, having lunches in the parks, going to the churches. But mostly, they stayed in Pino's little room. She didn't tell her parents about this and swore her maid to secrecy. And then, she had a baby."

"Before they got married?"

"Unfortunately, yes. Veronica didn't know what to do. The maid thought the parents should know so she told them. They were incensed. The father, Massimo, rushed to Bologna and threw Pino out. He then had a big fight with Veronica, but then he saw the baby. It was a beautiful little boy, who Veronica called Lorenzo. Massimo held the baby and kissed it. This, he thought, would be the heir to my riches."

"So it all ended happily?" Stefano said.

Nonno crumpled the wrapper from his *cornetto* and Stefano threw it in the nearby garbage can.

"No, not at all," Nonno said. "On the way back to San Ferdinando, robbers attacked their party. Massimo's bodyguard killed two of them but their carriage turned over. Massimo and Veronica escaped but little Lorenzo was crushed to death."

"Not happy at all."

"When they returned, Veronica changed her life. She dressed in black all the time and she went to church every day. She would go before the Mass and she would stay long after. She begged for forgiveness for her great sin."

"But she also missed the troubadour?"

"Well, yes, that, too."

"And she never saw him again?"

"Three years later, the Chiesa di Santa Zita planned a concert on the saint's feast day, April 27. They brought in a small chorus from Lucca, an ensemble from Pisa and a troubadour from Bologna."

"A troubadour! I know how this story ends already."

"Yes, Veronica recognized Pino and Pino recognized Veronica. They met after the concert. Massimo saw how much in love they still were and after thinking about it for a few days he allowed them to marry. A year later, they had a son, Angelo, the long-awaited heir to the Cappelli fortune."

"And so," Stefano said, "Angelo became the heir when his parents died and he had a son who had a son who had a son."

"No, I'm afraid not. Angelo decided to become a priest. He had no heirs."

"Bummer. So what happened to the house?"

"Angelo inherited it and turned it into a music school where they gave violin and cello and piano lessons. The Cappelli School of Music became famous all over Tuscany, and that's what it still is today. It's on the upper two floors and the *Panetteria* is on the first floor. There are many famous graduates who have gone on to play in symphony orchestras. Would you like to take lessons there, Stefano?"

"Me? No. I don't like music."

"You don't like music? What do you like?"

"I don't know. Just stuff."

"Oh. I think it's time to go home."

Almost no one was in the piazza now, only a few teenagers with headphones who were taking selfies. Clouds had started to form and were hiding the moon.

THE *PIZZERIA*

FESTA DELLA SANTA ZITA DI SAN FERDINANDO

STEFANO HATED IT when Vincenzo went on and on about stuff that Stefano knew nothing about. He was always talking about the old people he knew and things that happened a long time ago. Stefano closed his eyes and thought about something else, like the videogame he played the night before.

Now Vincenzo was always talking about that festival that was going to happen very soon, in August.

"It's going to be huge, Stefano. You're going to be amazed."

"Yeah, yeah."

"People are going to come from all over. Just wait."

"Yeah, yeah."

"It's the biggest thing to happen in San Ferdinando all year."

"Yeah, yeah."

At that point Stefano told Vincenzo that he had to go home. And he did.

After hearing about this great festival all summer, Stefano asked his grandfather about it.

"Well," Nonno said, finishing yet another basket, this one destined for Father Antonio, who said he wanted one for his golf balls. "The *Festa della Santa Zita di San Ferdinando* really is the biggest event in the village every year. It's famous."

"But what is it?"

Nonno started to answer, but thought better of it.

"Stefano, this time I'm not going to tell you the history. I'll just say the *festa* began in the Middle Ages and has been held every year on the first Saturday in August since, except for the time of the plague."

"Why won't you tell me more?"

"The *festa* is something you should discover for yourself. It's next Saturday so you won't have long to wait."

Nonno went back to his basket and Stefano stomped up to his room.

Besides the church bells, Stefano and Enrico were awakened on Monday morning by the sounds of heavy carts going over the cobblestones in the piazza. Running to the window, Stefano saw a line of wagons heading for the area in front of the *Pizzeria*.

"The *Pizzeria*!" He remembered that Vincenzo had told him that this would be the headquarters for the *Festa della Santa Zita di San Ferdinando*.

Workers unloaded eleven big boxes from the carts and stacked them in front of the *Pizzeria*. A flatbed delivered long poles to the center of the piazza and more workers placed them at equal distances around the perimeter. A truck brought large loudspeakers, and four electricians installed them on the highest buildings. Another carried big floodlights.

All the while, the men were singing. Loudly.

"What's going on, Grandfather?"

"They're starting to get ready for the *festa*. It's going to take all week."

In the following days, Stefano rarely left his perch on the doorstep to watch all the activity. It seemed as though there were hundreds of people unpacking the boxes of supplies, installing the loudspeakers and floodlights and erecting the poles that soon were strung with banners and garlands.

More workers set up tables in front of some of the buildings and out on the adjoining streets. Nonno explained that some tables were going to hold food, others were going to be used to demonstrate various arts and crafts from the Middle Ages.

Venturing down Via Giovanni Battista Bertini, Stefano found Vincenzo suddenly at his side.

"See, I told you, Stefano, this is going to be great."

"Yeah, yeah."

They watched as a brawny man in a canvas apron set up a wheel to sharpen knives. Next to him, two men, who could have been twin brothers, installed a straw shield for a bow and arrow exhibition. Four monks from a nearby abbey laid out parchment to demonstrate how books were made. An elderly woman spread out fine cloths that would be turned into dresses.

"See," Vincenzo said, "everything is like it was in the Middle Ages. It's going to be like we are going to be back in time, just like that *Lancelot* videogame we play."

Stefano was too engrossed in all of this to attempt a reply.

On Friday, as everyone was running back and forth, they came to the most exciting exhibit. A young man wearing heavy leather gloves unloaded two cages from a cart.

"What's in there?" Stefano asked.

"You'll see."

The man opened the cage and gently pulled out the most beautiful bird Stefano had ever seen, its wings every color of the rainbow and then some.

"It's a hawk," Vincenzo said. "He's going to fly it tomorrow."

The bird suddenly spread its wings and Stefano and Vincenzo jumped back.

"Don't worry," the man said. "He won't hurt you."

The man kissed the bird's beak, murmured something, and put it back in its cage. Then he opened the other cage and pulled out a small bird with a dark blue back and wings that matched the streaks on its white chest.

"That's a falcon. The guy is going to fly it. He's called a falconer. You'll see."

Stefano couldn't believe what he'd seen and rushed home to tell his mother, father and grandfather.

"You'd better sleep well tonight," his mother said. "You're going to have a lot of excitement tomorrow."

Stefano was awakened the next morning not by church bells or carts but by the shrill blasts of a bugle. Standing in the center of the piazza next to the well, a tall man in red, blue and white medieval garb was telling the world that the *Festa della Santa Zita di San Ferdinando* was about to begin. Almost immediately, the piazza was filled with men, women, children of all ages, singing and dancing. Dressed in medieval costumes, they looked like they'd stepped out of the pages of Stefano's beloved book.

"Mama! Mama! It's starting! I'm going to miss it!"

Stefano pulled off his pajamas and was getting dressed when his mother stopped him.

"Wait, Stefano. Look what's hanging on your closet door."

Stefano couldn't believe it. A smaller version of a flag thrower's outfit hung on a hanger, its silk tunic blue and white with a red tower emblazed on the front, dark blue tights underneath, red slippers on the floor.

"Who did that?" he cried. "Wow!"

"When you were at Vincenzo's I bought some cloth at a shop on Via Bandettini and sewed this together. Your father and grandfather helped, too. See the tower. This was the uniform of the *contrada* where we live, the *Contrada della Torre.*"

"The Tower! I know that! Nonno told me." Stefano hugged his mother and climbed into the costume.

"Looks like you're ready for the big day," his father said. "Let's go!"

Vincenzo was waiting at the doorstep. Like Stefano, he was dressed in a medieval costume, only his was red and white and had a black panther on the chest.

"I live in the *Contrada della Pantera,*" he said. "The Panther. Remember your grandfather telling us when we were at the museum?"

"Of course I remember. Your mother made that?"

"Yes! When I was at your house!"

The piazza was still filling with people from all over San Ferdinando. All were in the costumes according to the *contrada* where they lived, red and white, blue and white, orange and white, purple and white. Drummers were drumming, pipers were piping, buglers were blaring. A trio of teenage boys played a flute, a horn and a harp in one corner, mixing medieval church hymns with Twenty-first century rock. The church bells rang every hour on the hour.

In a space in front of Albergo Sant'Anna, a giant of a man spit roasted an entire boar, and the heavy aroma drifted across the piazza. In front of the *Gelateria,* a young couple fried apples in a cheese dough, which the woman told the boys was a delicacy called *frictella.* An ancient woman presided over a display of rare cheeses: *caciotta, pecorino, darraghetto di Viareggio, orrengigo di Pistola,* Near the palazzo, a mother, father and four children packaged a variety of sausages, salamella, mortadella, *soppressata* and salami for buyers to take away.

Since they hadn't had breakfast, Stefano and Vincenzo aimed for the *Panetteria* where two women in long blue dresses and white aprons and caps stood behind stacks of crusty hard breads and an array of goodies, not just *biscotti* and *pizzelle* and *cannoli,* all in many different flavors, but also *torcetti, amaretti, cuccidati,* sesame cookies, spritz cookies, honey clusters, horn cookies, anise and wine cookies, and even more.

After much deliberation, the boys each chose six different ones and planned to offer each other a bite. They sat on a bench to devour them.

"Cool, right?" Vincenzo asked.

"Yeah."

At 10 o'clock, the bugler took his place in front of the well and blasted another round. Everyone stopped talking and singing. A portly man dressed rather like a magistrate read from a scroll.

"*Gli Sbandieratori!*" he cried.

"What's happening?" Stefano asked Vincenzo.

"You'll see."

Four men marched in through the Porta Santa Maria. Each was in a different costume: blue and white with a red tower on his chest representing the *Contrada della Torre,* red and white with a black panther on his chest from the *Contrada della Pantera,* orange and white with a tortoise from the *Contrada della Tartaruga,* and purple and white with a large tree from the *Contrada della Selva.* Each carried a large flag with similar colors. They ran around the piazza to the cheers—and a few jeers—from the crowd.

"They're from the four *contrade* in San Ferdinando," Vincenzo said. "Now they're going to compete in flag throwing."

The competition, it turned out, was not nearly as precise or breathtaking as the performance of the *Sbandieratori dei Borghi e Sestieri Fiodrentini* that the boys had seen a few weeks earlier. In fact, these *sbandieratori* seemed to be having more fun than demonstrating any skills.

With much bowing and scraping to the onlookers and each other, they arranged themselves in four corners of the piazza. Bugles and drums announced the beginning of the performance, and *Tartaruga* threw his flag high in the air and *Selva* ran to catch it. Then *Torre* tossed his straight at *Pantera,* who caught it just before it struck a delicate region. The throngs yelled and laughed and jeered.

Then they changed places and tried to do individual acts, though the flags hit the cobblestones more often than they were caught.

"Go *Torre!*"

"Go *Pantera!*"

Each *contrada* had its cheering section and there were occasional loud arguments between them.

The only flag thrower with any talent seemed to be *Selva,* and the other three eventually yielded. He stood in the middle, flawlessly throwing his flag in the air, then under his arms and then his legs, and twirling it through various maneuvers. The crowd applauded again and again.

Finally, to loud cheers, all four ran around the edge and back through the Porta Santa Maria.

"Wow!" Stefano said. "That was fun. Now I know what my grandfather was laughing about. Now what?"

"I'm hungry. Let's have something to eat."

After inspecting a half dozen food stalls, they decided on the iconic *porchetta* sandwich, thick meat from a whole suckling pig, stuffed with herbs and placed between massive pieces of crusty bread. As a side dish they chose a bowl of *risotto* with pumpkin and rosemary. They finished both in record time and lay back on a bench, too stuffed to move and too sleepy to stay awake.

At 2 o'clock they were awakened by the bugler again and the magistrate stepped forward. "*Il Palio di San Ferdinando!*"

Both boys leapt to their feet. "Oh wow!"

They couldn't believe that actual horses would be in a palio in the piazza, and as it turned out, there weren't. One by one, young men in the costumes of *Torre, Pantera, Tartaruga* and *Selva* rode through the Porta Santa Maria—on donkeys. Small donkeys. Donkeys so small that the riders' feet dragged on the ground.

The crowd hooted and cheered. Stefano and Vincenzo laughed hysterically and bounced up and down.

True to palio fashion, the donkey riders lined up next to the *Pizzeria. Tartaruga's* donkey decided to turn backwards and *Torre's* relieved himself on the cobblestones, resulting in more hoots from the crowd.

Finally, they were ready. The bugler burgled and the race began. While the palio in Siena lasted less than two minutes and the one in medieval San Ferdinando was over in about five, this one went on and on as the donkeys decided to stop, turn around, go backwards and then sideways. More than once the rider had to get off and push a reluctant beast.

At last, *Pantera* made it back to the starting line and the mass of people swarmed upon its rider, carrying him in triumph all around the piazza where the other three riders were still trying to get their animals moving.

"Yeah, *Pantera!*" Vincenzo shouted. "I knew you could do it."

The crowd fell silent as the bugler bugled and the magistrate announced "*Processione di Santa Zita.*" It was time for the most solemn event of the *Festa della Santa Zita di San Ferdinando.* Stefano's parents and grandfather were at his side.

"You stay with us now, Stefano," his father said. "Vincenzo, you go with your parents."

"Why?" Stefano asked.

"You'll see."

A procession began to form in front of the church. First came the bugler, with three other buglers behind him. Then six drummers. Then a group of men in black bearing a banner declaring *Congregazione di Santo Paolo*, followed by another group identified as the *Congregazione di San Francesco*, and then the *Congregazione di Sant'Antonio*. Carrying white prayer books and rosaries, two dozen little girls in First Communion dresses followed.

Next came a dozen elderly women wearing black veils over their medieval gowns. Their banner read *Società di Santa Maria Goretti* and they sang the same hymn over and over:

O Sanctissima, O Piissima
Dulcis Virgo Maria
Mater amata, intemerata
Ora, ora pro nobis

Then a group of actors paid tribute to the medieval *Commedia dell'arte* performances with Pantolone, Colombina, the Doctor and Arlecchino dancing and singing and performing little skits to the amusement of the children.

"Arlecchino is my favorite," Stefano said, clutching his grandfather's hand.

"Mine, too."

Students from the school in *Palazzo del Duca di San Ferdinando* carried a banner that included depictions of their majors, a painting of a computer and another of a stove. A dozen drummer boys followed. After a pause, a float pulled by four men carried six violin students from the Cappelli School of Music playing a Vivaldi concerto.

There were more groups, more bands. It seemed as though everyone in San Ferdinando had a part in the procession. The *Congregazione di San Baudalino*. The *Congregazione di San Bernardino*. *The Società di Santa Michelina*. The *Società di Santa Silvia*. Each had its own hymn. The sun was setting and the first stars appeared. A group of altar boys and girls carried lighted candles.

A long pause made some observers anxious, but then a tall burly man appeared. He was about forty years old with his hair in a ponytail and a beard that hadn't been shaved in several days. Over one shoulder he carried a pole with a beautiful, if faded, silk banner decorated with a shield, an arrow, a lion and a book.

"Mama, Papa, Nonno!" Stefano cried. "It's Carlo Roberto!"

The descendant of Duke Carlo and Lucia recognized Stefano and his family and went over to greet them.

"Are you having fun, Stefano?"

"Sure. But where's Sweetie? Is she OK?"

"Sweetie? She's fine, but she hates crowds."

Then came the climax and the crowd fell silent. Six strong men pulled a cart covered with flowers. On it, surrounded by more flowers, the statue of Saint Zita wobbled a little but eventually stood firm. Except for a crown of lights and flowers, she looked the same as in the church. Those along the route rushed to toss hundreds of *euro* bills into a big bucket in front of her.

Following the cart to the church, the crowd overflowed far into the piazza. Saint Zita was returned to her altar, and, with a large, newly formed choir, Father Antonio said the Mass wearing brilliant gold vestments. Skipping a homily, he simply said: "May God bless us, may Saint Zita pray for us, and may we all help and love each other. Enjoy the rest of the *Festa della Santa Zita di San Ferdinando.*"

In other words, it was time to eat again. The piazza was now lit by the floodlights, tall candles around the booths and cell phones. Papa, Mama, Nonno and Stefano visited the pasta booth and came away with bowls of fettuccine, pappardelle, ravioli and tortellini. A couple of teenagers gave up the bench where they were taking selfies and the family settled down. Stefano couldn't finish his tortellini.

"Stuffed?" his father asked.

"Yes."

"I was going to have a gelato," Nonno said. "Want one?"

"Not tonight."

"Stefano!" his mother said. "This is the first time in your life that you've refused ice cream."

"I know. But I'm stuffed."

"And sleepy," his father said. "But there's one more thing in the festival."

Behind the bell tower, a skyrocket burst toward the yellow moon.

"Boom!"

"Oh, wow!"

A burst with falling stars. One that looked like a peony. Another like a palm. A fish. A chrysanthemum. A crossette. Sometimes two or three were together, sometimes one after another. Stefano covered his ears but stood motionless and never took his eyes away from the spectacular display in the skies.

"OK," Papa said after the final spectacle. "Time to go home."

Leaving behind a string band playing outside the *Pizzeria* and a few couples dancing al fresco, they walked across the piazza to the house they now called home. Stefano could hear the music and the laughter as he took off his *Contrada della Torre* costume, gathered Enrico and climbed into bed. A minute later, Nonno entered.

"Aren't you glad we moved to San Ferdinando, Stefano?"

The boy smiled in his sleep.

The author and his grandfather (circa 1940).

Printed in the United States
By Bookmasters